They Didn't Eat Me for Supper

Roxanne Remy

 B.F.F.

THEY DIDN'T EAT ME FOR SUPPER

For conent warnings view:

http://www.roxanneremy.com
Book and Cover design by Tatiana Vila at Vila Design Book Cover Images
ISBN: 978-1-7364917-8-2
First Edition: July 2022

All cruelty springs from weakness.
-Seneca

PROLOGUE

Lennon

There's peace in death, my mother tells me.

And why shouldn't I trust her? In decades of nursing, she's witnessed the end through the eyes of countless. She's held the hands of war veterans fighting their last battle. She was the caretaker dabbing loved ones' cracked lips when COVID stripped families from bedsides. Even as a parent, my mother experienced the quiet redemption of a child. Kristin Murphy knows death, and she vows it's as peaceful as the wings of the arriving angel.

When nightmares drifted into my mind, I, like most kids, felt comforted knowing she'd slain bigger dragons. As a teen, when visions of my demise polluted my brain, Mom taught me thoughts are merely mental whispers to be believed or dismissed at my discretion. Her constant message reassured me: fear is absent in the end. According to her, Dad's death was swift; his suffering didn't exist. His mind was calm. His breathing, easy. His muscles released their tension as neurotransmitters sent messages between his brain and vital organs. Her medical rationale satiated my worries as a child. Although I've done my own research since then, and my naivety is long gone.

The truth is, his sympathetic nervous system took over as an initial response. Within minutes, he experienced profuse sweating and body tremors, followed by profound anxiety. It's often called a sense of impending doom. Given his body processed an extraordinary dose of medication, his vision swirled him into a pit of nausea and unfathomable confusion. By that point, the police report confirmed, he likely wanted to call for help, but was too disoriented to dial the numbers 9-1-1.

The electrical-communication system of my father's body collapsed soon after, but not before he experienced full-body thrashing, sending his tall, sturdy frame to the hotel room floor, a dresser breaking his fall. A sanguineous flood covered the grey matter fissures of his brain, ultimately pooling at the base. Bone plates expanded to accommodate the increasing pressure; however, brain real estate is a premium. Soft tissue shifted and blood filled the void until the immune system retaliated enough to clot the flow. Maybe this is the point where Hutch Camek's suffering eased. My mother said our bodies are designed to protect us until the end; she forgot to mention his end was designed by her.

CHAPTER ONE

Lennon

After hours on the road, driving into our hometown is anything but welcoming. My roommate acknowledges our arrival with a horn honk crossing over the city limits.

"It feels good to see that sign," Taylor says, leaning forward to stretch their lower back. "We should have flown."

"*You* could have."

"Meaning, *you* didn't want to accept the plane ticket your family offered."

"Too many strings attached," I say. "Besides, I thought you liked our road trips."

Awaiting their response, I stare at the blurred hibiscus-colored layers rising from the horizon. Mixed herds of cattle pass outside my window like chocolate chips scattered over the rich, hilly farmlands from my youth. Several crowd together under the eaves of pecan trees next to twisted barbed wire. As the morning greets them, they dig their elbows into the earth and rock their massive bodies until they're steady on all four hooves. The sunlight glares through our windshield. I flip the visor and my eyes focus on my parents' perfectly blended hand-me-down lying across my chest. The strawberry highlights pop against my denim jacket almost taking over the blonde. I lift my strands feeling them break free from the collar. The familiar odor of farm animals wafts through the air vents, forcing me to hold my breath until it passes.

"I like our drives when there's breaks and snacks and music. But you didn't want any of that."

Forced air puffs my lips. "Sorry, this isn't a pleasurable trip for me. I helped with driving this time," I say, keeping my friend focused on our mission.

"On a nineteen-hour road trip?" Their voice raises an octave. "I should hope the hell you did."

"*And* I paid for the hotel in Atlanta. It wasn't cheap either. The breakfast bar had the little waffle maker you like."

My friend flashes a sideways smirk. "I do love those waffles."

Their response makes my cracked lips pinch into a forced smile, and I'm reminded to retrieve the tube of lip balm from my front pocket.

"Do we need to discuss your strategy before we get to the hospital?" Taylor asks.

"I'm going to see my sister. What's to discuss?"

"And?"

I pause watching the blonde-brown ringlets of my friend's hair coil around their tightened jaw, their glare fixed on the road ahead. "I'm going to find out who's poisoning her," I mumble.

"Now there's the Lennon Camek I've known and loved for... how many years now?"

"Too many."

They smirk. "Admit it. You've come up with some wild schemes, *Leonard*." They nudge me with their elbow. "Can we discuss this plan of yours?"

"When we get to the hospital, we'll stay with Liv until she wakes up and can tell us who's trying to kill her."

"Okay, and what do we do until she's able and, need I add, willing to speak to us? Should I stand guard at the bedside while you look for clues?"

I nod yes in silence recognizing an ad for my family's feed and seed store on the local radio. "Huh. They're open on Sunday's now, after church of course." I wave my finger in the air.

"Focus, please."

My head snaps in their direction before returning to my window view. "I'm still working on some holes."

Taylor tsks. "The *whole* thing is a hole!" Their nostrils flare. "I'm sorry, I know you have a big heart. It's just sometimes your ideas get you...us...into a pinch, my girl. We have to use some caution; legally we're adults now."

My eyes burn as tears pool in my lower lids for what feels like the thousandth time today.

"What makes you so sure someone's hurting Liv? You've not talked to anyone in your family in over a year, not your stepdad, not your sister, and certainly not your mom. How do you know what's going on in her life right now?"

"I know my sister. She's a senior in high school, Division One tennis athlete, honor roll student, Homecoming Queen. Basically, she's everything I'm not."

"And, she has diabetes."

"She's hospitalized for a low blood sugar coma," I say. "At least that's what your mom reported when she called us yesterday."

My friend shrugs their shoulders. "I'm not a diabetic, but I can't imagine it's easy functioning like a human organ. Liv's battled this disease since she's been ten. She may have had a rough go this week. Even the most compliant diabetics can have a bad blood sugar day, week, month."

"I'm not buying it."

"I don't think she's *selling* anything."

We fall silent again and my breath fogs the glass. "There's more to it," I say, forcing my eyes to cross, staring at the tiny crystals on the window. Warmth dribbles down my cheek. "Let's talk about your mom, instead. How's Aunt Tish managing the whole non-binary thing?"

"Don't change the subject," Taylor says, retrieving their gold aviators from the dashboard and sliding them into place to combat the morning glare.

"I appreciate the help getting a plan together. And, yes, I'll admit, I've had some big plans in the past—"

"*Big*, big."

"But I need more time to figure this Liv-situation out. Your issue is...simpler."

"It is pretty easy."

"If we can solve one dilemma, maybe our brains will come up with a solution for the other."

Taylor's chest expands and releases. "Moms seems cool with everything. She's trying to use my preferred pronouns more. It takes time, I get it. Now back to you."

"Wait, what? That's it?"

"I told you, Moms'll be aight'. You and I need to be on the same page when we get to the hospital, or she'll know we're up to something."

"You said, 'we're,'" I smirk. "So, you'll help me?"

"I'll make sure Liv's safe. She's like my sister too."

"Well, I'm open to suggestions. I've never tried to pin attempted murder on my mother before."

"Uh, you've totally tried to pin murder on her before," they say. "The child endangerment angle is a new twist."

"Was I wrong about her then?" I jerk my head in their direction, widening my eyes.

"Not wrong, but if anything, you learned to let the authorities handle things."

"Well, we see where the authorities left it, don't we?" I ask. "I need your help in determining a motive. Why would a mother want to kill her own child? Her ex-husband...was easy to prove, but her own daughter?"

"I..."

"What?"

"Nothing." They shake their head, and pull their plump lips in with their teeth.

"Say it. Like I have to ask you to speak your mind. We've been best friends since first grade."

"I just don't think Aunt Kris has anything to do with this."

We sit in silence as a familiar burning sensation returns to my chest. I lace my fingers together in my lap and contemplate why my friend pretends not to know the real story. Not the one we were told as children, nor the version that the town believes. The confession shared with me when I confronted Dad's killer in jail over a year ago. "I've told you everything I know."

"You have. It's just—"

"First, Mom lied to me and Olivia by telling us Dad's death was a suicide. Then—"

"She said the arrest was for tax evasion," they say, rolling their eyes.

"Exactly! So, why press me about suspecting Mom is behind my sister's hospitalization? You know, I'm not being unreasonable."

"It's jacked up, not gonna lie. But I can't see Aunt Kris hurting Olivia. I mean, she's confessed to some shady shit, but I don't think this is her doing."

My elbows straighten pressing the heel of both palms as I fold my fingertips over the frayed edge of the upholstered seat. Gritting my teeth, I say, "Two people followed Dad into an elevator after he left his company's party in the hotel conference room." I force a swallow. "When the doors closed..." My voice raises. "A couple started arguing. The tall one fell into Dad." Short, choppy breaths rattle drainage in the back of my throat. "My dad was no chump; he puffed up." I release my grip on the seat and throw two sharp air punches toward the windshield, drawing a scowl from my driver. "The other short, chunky one popped his 'side meat' with a needle." I slam my hand in my fist, then pinch Taylor above their waistband. "Right here."

"Ouch! Dammit, Lennon that hurt," they say, swatting my hand. "Why are you telling me this? I know what happened to your father."

Paste forms over my tongue. I sip my Mountain Dew from earlier; the lukewarm fizz gags me. "Syringes have tiny needles, but it doesn't take much medicine to cause organ shut down. The police said Dad likely felt the prick, but he was focused on getting the drunk guy off him." I toss the half-empty bottle onto the pile of clothes behind our seats.

"You gonna put that in the trash when we stop."

"The next morning, the housekeeper found him on the floor."

"Yes. May he rest in peace. I didn't know him, but I'm sure Mr. Camek didn't deserve to die like that."

"My mother hired someone to kill him," I say, holding my hand in the air and pulling a finger back with each fact. "She's a nurse.

She has access to medications. Kristin Murphy clearly knows patho, pathophys—"

"It's just weird when musicians try to use medical phrases."

"The human body, yet you still give her the benefit of the doubt when it comes to Olivia."

"It's been five years, Lennon. Aunt Kris paid for her mistakes. When do you start to forgive?"

"When my dad hugs me again, how long is that?"

Taylor shakes their head. "Moms says, when Aunt Kris lost custody of you and Olivia, she had a nervous breakdown. Her world crumbled when the judge ordered you to move to Lake Tarpon. And then Olivia followed. " They smack their lips together, and say, "The situation is different this time. She's done years of therapy and rehabilitation. Aunt Kris made a mistake, but she's not a serial killer."

"What if she's relapsed?" I ask, looking away.

"There's no guarantee." The stoplight changes to green, and my friend hesitates to move forward. "You can never replace your father, I get it. But why lose two parents over this? Maybe it's time to forgive her, Len."

Our car inches ahead. I stare at the tattered tailgate of the farm truck in front of us. Taylor may be right, but I can't risk losing my sister by doing nothing.

CHAPTER TWO

Lennon

My stomach churns as hills roll into a drab white building in the distance. The rising sun washes one side into bleakness. The others are darkened by shade still awaiting warmth. Lamps glow in windows on every floor. We pass corridors of medical offices and an outpatient surgery center toward the main entrance. The red cross beacons to weary drivers and directional arrows glow a path toward the emergency room. Air washes through me until my lungs are fully stretched. Acres of soybean fields fade in the background, and I remind myself: leaving this dump was the best decision I've made in all my nineteen years.

A woman I've known for most of those years stands outside.

"Damn, Moms already saw us. You'd think we'd get a minute to get our shit together," Taylor says. "Seven a.m. came early for college *sophomores*. It still feels weird to say that."

I can't argue. I'm surprised we survived our first year at Berklee. Even more so, we're allowed to come back. "Well, the Tay-tor Tot is hard to miss," I say.

"It got your behind where it needed to be, didn't it?" Taylor asks, with full focus on every corner of their latte-brown Kia Soul, their mother doing the same. "How does my parking look on that side?"

"I mean, does it matter? This car's suffered through your parking for three years, two high school proms, and one Boston winter." My friend cuts a scowl in my direction. "You're in the lines."

11

"Ungrateful, I tell you." Taylor shakes their head, reaching into the door pocket beside them. "Un-grateful," they mumble. My friend's gaze fixes past me, and I already know the offer. "You wanna hit this?"

Their fingers tilt the silver pen in my direction. A hit before going in feels like the next best thing I can do. "You watching your mom?"

"Yup," Taylor answers, following their response with a turbulent cough.

The inhale scorches.

Hold it. One-two-three.

Smoke whispers through my nose and more thoughts flood.

How am I going to get through today?

Taylor takes the pen back as I mirror their raspy cough knowing this stream of fire is the best feeling I'll experience today.

"Let's go before she walks over here," they say.

The car spins; their direction escapes me. "It came on fast."

"Hey, let's go," Taylor says with widened eyes, tapping the window.

Pushing the door open, sunlight reflects off my ring. Olivia and I received identical ones at birth, both designed for us to grow into. The infinity symbol shimmers around a single pearl reminding us: a sister's bond is unbreakable.

My foot stretches on to the pavement. "Where's the parking meter?" my friend asks, scanning the line of rooftops on either side of the car.

"Home is good for something, I guess."

"Yeah, free parking anywhere you go. It's just..."

"There's nowhere to go," we say, in unison. Our silliness forces a half-ass laugh from my lips, which is the most I've done in two days. A blast of cool air lifts my hair into a mini cyclone until I'm completely tangled. Using my tongue, I push persistent strands from my mouth and close the door with my hip.

"Look at 'L.A.' trying to compete with Back Bay. I'm glad I brought a fleece. Hold up." Taylor's voice strains with their reach. "Let me get it out the back."

Fall in lower Alabama is far from Boston's. Evergreen needled branches hang, reminding me why I ran from here a year ago. Now, street sounds replace humming katydids on my morning walks for coffee. Sleek architectural pillars hug my path, not kudzu-tangled honeysuckle vines. The occasional stench of warm garbage, waiting for pickup on the sidewalk, is welcomed over cow fields and chicken coops pummeled with manure. Any other day, I'd enjoy my new morning ritual of sipping tea in bed, overlooking the rooftops along Belvedere up to the Prudential, but today I'm back to face a reality I've avoided.

Aunt Tish stands in front of glass doors etched with Saint Luke's cross. Or is it Saint Mark? Hell, they're all saints compared to me. Leticia Piedmont has been in my family for as long as I can remember. She's one of those non-blood-related aunts, but I'd never say that to her. I'm not surprised she's the one who called. She probably hasn't left the bedside, which is right where Mom wants her.

My eyes squint reading her facial expression as she emerges from the building's shadows. A strong buzz numbs my senses, I can't make out her reaction. Her taupe sweater drapes over her round hips, touching the edge of her camel leather booties. She tucks her hand beneath the sweater's edge, pulling her t-shirt tight across her chest. The cardigan slips farther down her shoulder, exposing the capped sleeve and brilliant white that pops against her midnight skin. Despite the fall blast, it's no surprise she's meeting the bare minimum for warmth. She says she's been in a permanent hot flash since 1993. Her ebony waves layer across her forehead, fanning, in rhythm with the opening doors behind her. The white doves of the hospital logo meet in tandem with the gray along her parting. My choice to have a quick smoke in the car haunts me.

Get a grip, Lennon.

I sharpen my focus on the blinding smile I've not seen for many months. Her pale pink lip gloss shimmers: I'd worry if it was plumb.

"Well, well, look what the cat dragged in," she says, shifting her stance. "Two of Berklee's finest musicians, right here in Ellington, Alabama."

"Producer, Moms. Len makes the music; I make it good enough for the world to hear it," Taylor says, moving their hands around an invisible orb.

"Oh, I see how it is. Ay!" Tish says, dropping into her jutted hip. "Paint your world baby girl, we're just lucky to be in it."

"They/them, Moms. We've talked about the pronouns I prefer."

"They? The—Producer Tay, you better hug your mama, right now."

Aunt Tish's laugh still slaps. Open mouth and wide tongue, and not a care for anybody or anything watching her. She clutches her child, and a tinge of jealousy tenses my brow. I step away to give them room to sway, noticing Tish's gray strands run deeper than I first thought or I've been away from home longer than I realize.

"Come over here, my 'calla lily.'" Her body wraps around me like a familiar blanket and my heart aches recalling the last time I felt this safe.

"Is that a new body spray?"

"Yes, child. Gardenia Fields was on clearance at Bath and Body. I snuck over there between clients yesterday. Which reminds me, when are y'all coming by the shop?" she asks, running her fingertips through my frayed strands.

I know where this is going, so I step back and punt. "Tay's driving."

"I don't need anything," Taylor says, cutting their fawny green eyes in my direction. Their eyelashes bristle across their bronze cheek for my friend's signature look.

"Did you just say—" Their mother returns said signature look, and it's clear who Tay inherited it from.

"Oh, sh—" I finish in a whisper. My lips pull together, and I slowly lean toward the ground to buff my boots.

"Are you *actually* standing in front of the woman who gave life to them, thy, they—" she says, giving her feathered bangs a firm shake. "*You*, with the Lord's graces, saying these two dried-out pom-poms on the top of your head don't need *anything*?" Tish's nude-painted nails surround one of the ponytails on my friend's head like an eagle's talon, pulling it in for a closer look. Her rich brown eyes scour it as Taylor's hands flail over their head.

"Ouch! Moms, really? You gonna pick through my hair, here?"

"What kind of cheap box dye did you try?" She jerks Taylor's head toward her scowl again. "Is this supposed to be purple?"

"Violet," Tay says. "What? Hair salons are expensive in Boston."

I pray they don't say what I think is next.

"Besides, Lennon put it on for me," they say, narrowing their eyes in my direction again.

I release a loud sigh. "I was trying to keep you from making a big mistake. I..." My weight shifts on my ankles and I look to the ground; Aunt Tish's icy stare scans me from tip to tail. Resting my hands over by heart I continue, "I, of all people, understand the value of good hair products."

"Lennon Rosalyn, you just keep getting cleverer by the damn day, don't you?"

"Jus' sayin'."

"Jus—jus' sayin' what? Let me get to you next." Tish's palm has stopped me in my tracks for a lifetime. "Taylor Ragin Piedmont, don't you leave this town without letting me cut that mess out of your hair. You need a hot oil treatment and some leave-in conditioner to take back with you; I just bought all the Oyin products the beauty supply had in stock."

"Oh, I do love that brand." My friend's eyes widen as they give a firm nod to release their top knot from Aunt Tish's clutches.

"Your mama knows what you like," she says. "Now you, Miss Clever Music Writer, what have I told you about conditioning that haystack?"

"I don't remember."

"You wha— Well, let me jog your memory. Your mother brought you to my shop, you were...how old?" She rolls her eyes toward the sky, then back toward the ground before placing both hands on her hips. "No, you were younger. Because Taylor had just started first grade when they came home talking about a new 'sister' at school."

How about we just not reminisce at all today?

"Anyways, you was little. Your mom and I met at a birthday party the weekend before. When we realized you and Taylor had a class together, we chatted it up. You know Mom-talk," she says, flipping her wrist in my direction. "Well, one day she'd had all she could take with that hair of yours, child." She slaps her thigh with her hand. "Kris remembered I had a shop across town. When she hit that salon door, all I could see was her red eyes looking at me from behind a worn-out, twisted tissue. Your knotty hair-self bounced inside my shop, and you gave a big smile as soon as you saw Tay."

"You still do that when you see me," my best friend says.

"Ay!" Tish squeals, closing her eyes. "Your hair had her in a tizzy. She'd tried coconut oil, horse mane conditioner, mayonnaise, you name it."

"Mayonnaise?" Taylor screeches.

"Straight-haired girl problems, I guess," I say, smirking.

"It was!" Aunt Tish bellows another hearty laugh, giving a firm nod. "I told her you needed leave-in conditioner, not a leg reattached. I got her a glass of wine from the back fridge; she sat her behind in the chair and learned from the master." Her hair flips in the wind while she continues to boast. "We lathered your hair, put on a shower cap, and you and Taylor played while I joined her with a glass of my own."

You've been best friends ever since.

"She's been my best friend ever since."

"Okay, conditioner. I'll get some at the store before we leave town," I say, hoping this walk down memory lane takes a detour.

"You need more than a store brand cream rinse," says Taylor.

My eyes widen and I tilt my chin. *Bruh, I'm higher than an Alabama pine, and you want me to take notes on beauty advice.*

"All those years of flat ironing in middle school, trying to hide your daddy's curls, has caught up with you," Tish says.

"It's just, we're not able to stay long." My jaw clenches.

"You're testing my blood pressure meds today, I see." Tish rests her hand over her chest. "Lucky for you, they're working. My hand to God, your mama would have my—"

"Well, she's not here, is she?" My throat tightens, and another raucous cough forces through my airway.

Tish tilts her head, shifting her coal-colored layers over her shoulder. "Come *here.*"

My eyes dart sideways looking for a drink machine. "It's okay," I say, backing away from her extended arms.

"Come here." Her fingertip points to me, then to the space in front of her.

Please don't do this, Aunt Tish. Hugging you will make me feel everything I've run from since graduation.

She steps toward me. The smell of gardenias folds me into her pillowy chest, and I don't think I'll be able to let go. My shoulders tense because: I don't want to cry again, I don't want to hear Mom still loves me, and I don't want to be lied to anymore. I raise my face to see her head reared back, with her eyes closed speaking to someone I cannot see, but I've felt near to me before. My forehead rests on her shoulder and I long to return to my mind-numbing life twelve hundred miles from here.

"I know this is hard, baby girl," she says, resting her chin on my scalp. "And it's about to get worse when you walk through those doors."

CHAPTER THREE

Lennon

Tish's hugs take me back to when my chest didn't ache from smoking or heartbreak.

I'm relieved she doesn't bring up my poor decisions or twisted paths. Maybe this is the part where she tells me this isn't happening. And none of it is my fault: My dad didn't die because of my incessant whining as a child, and my sister's life isn't resting in the balance of a madwoman I abandoned her to. I inch out a muffled acknowledgment to Tish's warning as she pushes me from her embrace.

"Both of you, listen." Stepping back, she grips Taylor's hand and mine. "Olivia will be fine, but she's in a bad way right now. It won't be easy to see her."

"I've seen her sick before," I say, reassuring Tish as much as myself. "She's been in and out of doctor's offices all of her life."

"I understand, but you haven't been home for a year, and she's struggled keeping her health in check, physical and emotional."

"Moms, can I go in the room with Len?"

A surge of adrenaline pulses through me hearing Taylor keep our plan on track.

"Let's see how many visitors they're allowing in today. Y'all come with me."

Tish's satin palms fold around my cracked hands, and she leads me somewhere I do not want to go. The swoosh from the sliding doors smells like tragedy mixed with bleach. You know they're covering something up. I understand how my mom worked here for so long; she fits right in.

"Fourth floor."

Taylor's chipped, black polish hovers over the button, and the doors shut. With each passing level, I'm closer to everything I run from. Here, everyone knows everybody's business. Even though my family drama was years ago, it's a topic the locals pounce on with hopes of hearing a new tragedy arise.

Ding. The crisp smell of masked despair hits me in the face again.

"The phone automatically dials the reception desk," Tish says, nodding toward the olive-green telephone on the wall. "Len...Vy's working today."

Of course, she is. My day couldn't get any worse. I nod, staring before picking up the receiver. The handle is as cold as the woman who'll answer.

"PICU, Vy," she says, stretching her one-syllable name into two.

My mouth fills with air, and I cradle the phone with a clank.

"What's wrong? She didn't answer?"

"I can't do this. I mean, it's *Vy.*" I raise my palms to the ceiling. "I haven't talked to her since—"

"Baby, I know your challenges. You have every right to still be angry about your father's death. It was...a tragedy."

I force a swallow and dart my eyes to the tiled floor.

"But the police cleared them of the matter entirely. I've known Vy and Weyman, your stepdad...all the Murphies longer than I've known you or your mother; they're good people."

The drab floor swirls.

"Vy can seem heartless at times," Tish says, looking around the waiting room. "Hell, it's rumored she ran over her neighbor's cat because it used her gardenia pots as a litter box." Her hand rests on my shoulder. "But she's no hitman."

"The video—"

"Showed a tall person and a short—"

"Fat."

"*Heavy-set* accomplice. It was *possibly* a female given the fur trim around the hat."

"They were at the same conference as Dad."

"As were hundreds of people, and Vy and Weyman didn't know your mom's ex-husband. I've heard the evidence. They had an alibi. Besides, you already know the person who confessed was arrested," Tish says, leaning forward and placing her hand on my shoulder. "Please, put these feelings behind you before they get in the way of the real reason you're here." Her eyes darken. "The young girl who needs you, is right inside those doors." Pushing away, she asks, "Do you want me to call for you?"

I nod yes, handing Tish the receiver, wishing she could take every ounce of fear and anger boiling my blood.

"Vy? Tish...she's got a visitor...it's none of your *damn* business who it is. I swear, woman, I've known you my whole life, but you're nosier in your old age. Open the door or I will—"

Buzz. Clank. The bar pushes in with a clangorous shift and my heart skips.

"Tay, you comin'?" I ask, wrenching both hands together.

They look at their mother. "We'll come to the room later." Tish pats Taylor's hand. The corners of my friend's lips tuck into their cheeks. "You need to do this on your own."

"Will she even know I'm in the room?"

Tish nods. Through her pursed lips, she says, "She'll know."

"What if she wakes up?"

"Call the nurse."

"What if she doesn't? What if she just stays asleep?"

"Just be with her." Taylor shrugs their shoulders. "You don't have to say anything, if you don't want. She'll know you're there."

My neck rolls to each side pulling my shoulders back. Another clang unlocks memories of the dull green tiles passing beneath my boot soles. Sometimes, I skipped through the entry, holding hands with my sister on our way to visit our mother at the nurses' station. Other times, my heart was all that skipped, fearing what lurked behind the glass doors. On those trips, Mom or Dad held my hand. I'm the adult today, but I certainly don't feel like it. My pulse quickens in rhythm with the blinking halogen light above me.

The morning sun streams through a picture window, brightening the pediatric intensive care unit where my mother worked as a nursing instructor for many years. I approach the U-shaped console of the reception desk noticing they refreshed the faded mural. Frequent fliers and long-term admits added artwork between taking gruesome meds and excruciating treatments. It is a nice attempt to cover the sadness. Visitors enjoy a wall of daffodils painted by children, I get it. But when suffering seeps through, the rainbows fade and painted petals dull all over again. God forbid people think about the real reason they're here; they'd rather cover it up with smiling puppies. My sole drags, leaving a black streak behind my path.

Room numbers inch closer. Feet huddle beneath the pulled green-and-white striped curtains. A set of tawny, leather shoes identify the medical student in the room; they still dress to impress. They're close to the low-heeled navy pumps. That's the doc telling the family their options. Even if they know the child won't leave here alive, they're hiding it. They don't want to have that conversation until all options are explored.

Hope is essential within these walls. It's what drove my stepdad to build a wheelchair ramp, despite his daughter never using it. Just the thought of her coming home kept his heart together until Browning's final hours. Without hope, he would have crumbled much sooner.

The medical team held the truth from Mom and Grey, probably knowing the child would never survive the injuries she'd sustained in the wreck. It's all the same with these hospitals: A cheerful painting along the center wall, boring curtains, drab floors, and the wrenching sound of heartache whispering through this tomb.

This morning, staff in matching powder-blue scrubs hustle around the horseshoe-shaped desk with various tasks. An older woman stands at the end adjusting the glasses on the edge of her nose. Her routine intrigues me; she leans back, reads the monitor, pecks a touchscreen with her ringed fingers, then scans a tiny pill-filled bag before laying it beside her. She stops, cross-checks the computer, then resumes inventorying the next item. My mind wanders thinking how I can schmooze her away from her tasks and lift a baggie. The relief is temporary, but I'd welcome the escape today.

"Let me read this back to you to be sure I have it right," a woman says. The familiar screeching shivers me. Her rounded back barely visible behind the counter. "One to two milligrams of Ativan intravenous every four hours P-R-N. Titrate the Diprivan. Wean, as tolerated."

She stands, removing her reading glasses and pushing her fuchsia-tipped bangs to one side. The dishwater-blonde dulls her rainbow highlights, and I turn away feeling her glare burn into the back of my head. "Okay, I'll get this to the pharmacy. Wait, which doctor signed off on the order? Waters? Got it." The receiver clangs on the desk. "Residents," she says, huffing. "Lennon, is that you?"

I continue walking and evaluating more shoe positions under the curtains along my path.

"Len, it's Aunt Vy."

I'm jarred from my mental merry-go-ground of repeating the room number, and it slips out of my mind. Recreational activities in college, coupled with ADHD, aren't helping me today. I submit to her greeting by flashing a peace sign from my hip. "Hi."

"I colored my hair since I last saw you. And lost some weight," she says, twirling behind the desk. "What'd you think?"

My head tilts to the room next to me.

"Your mom—"

I shake off her next statement. "You know who I'm here to see. Where's my sister?"

Her pudgy finger points toward the next room on the right. My lungs fill and release. At least, the curtain is open.

Stepping inside, I tug the drape. The slow clinking along the metal rod fades Vy's rigid brow of my view. The lack of muscle movement in her face, leads me to suspect she's received a fresh dose of Botox.

Another dull backdrop becomes my focal point as I procrastinate seeing the girl in the hospital bed behind me. Mechanical clanks fill the room. Fire trickles down my throat, a reminder my attempt to numb my pain failed miserably. Prickling fingertips force me to squeeze my hands into fists.

One. Two. Three.

I lug my legs into position again, wishing I considered the amount of walking I'd do in these boots.

Gut punch.

Olivia lies covered in a twisted spaghetti of tubes and wires. Blinking holds my tears in my eyes. I creep closer to the edge of the bed. Resting on the bumpy-edged rail, I distance myself and watch her chest rise and fall at a robot's command.

A bent tube connects her lips to the bot. Spit collects in a pool in the plastic elbow, shifting back and forth with each blast. V-shaped tape pulls her mouth and jaw together. Liv's perfectly straight teeth rest above and beneath a stiff plastic tube. The rosy, plump lips that once roused my jealousy, and started 99% of our fights, look like two Saltines gaping around an oversized straw. Bags of fluids hang overhead, each with its own pathway into her motionless body. A rolled white towel supports her otherwise flaccid head, and I lose myself in her blankness.

My thoughts race: why does she need this medicine draining into her veins? Where's her glucose monitor? She likes to wear it on her arm. And her insulin pump, should be on her stomach. Pinching the sheet, I peer underneath hoping not to find either on her leg. She says those sites are the most painful. It doesn't take long to determine her lifesaving equipment isn't misplaced. There's hardly a muscle for her to inject on these twigs. Is this the same athlete I left a year ago? Should I ask Vy to check the room number again? This girl looks...sick. The fireball blonde I knew ate girls like this for breakfast.

This isn't how our relationship is supposed to end. My mother and this stupid ass disease are taking my sister from me. My lip quivers.

"I'm not losing you, too."

A single tear plops onto Liv's top sheet. My sleeve drags against the broken skin surrounding my nostrils forcing a groan.

Resuming my search for her insulin, the starched sheet falls into position, and I graze the needle secured to the back of her hand.

"Shit," I say. "Sorry, Liv." A firm cough releases a lodged plug from the back of my throat. If I've found my voice, I might as well use it. Mom said hearing was the last sense people lose.

"I hate you have to deal with this fucking asshole of a disease, sis. You don't deserve this. Hell, *I* don't deserve this!" I suck air through my nose and force a swallow. "I'm supposed to be at a party right now, making out with some fire-hot frat. How is this fair for either of us?" A muffled laugh clanks around in my chest and I use my cuff of my sleeve to dry my eyes. "If Mom is behind this...I'm here to get answers. Your big sis is here. Nothing can hurt you, now." My voice weakens wondering which one of us needs the reminder.

I remove my jacket, hanging it on the back of a nearby chair. Dammit, there goes the snot again. I scan the bleak walls for the standard-issue plastic container with white tissue pulled through the oval opening; these rooms are all set up the same. Liv and I played in the empty ones when Mom checked on things in the unit on her day off. Spotting a container by the sink, my feet clunk across the room. A firm rub with a crisp tissue sends a rush of sandpaper wrapped in gasoline across my upper lip.

"What's with this ratty-ass hospital? They *still* don't have a decent tissue in the place," I say, hoping Liv will have a witty comeback.

Her helpless image returns me to the sink to wash my hands. Splashing water seeps through my T-shirt to my stomach and the icy singe jerks my head up. I catch a glimpse of myself through the dried water spots on the mirror. "Wow, my hair *is* a haystack. You know, Aunt Tish came at me," I ramble, looking over my shoulder. "She's not wrong." I alternate cheeks in the return view while noticing the butterscotch flecks in my eyes people are always complimenting. "This waterproof mascara is living up to its hype. If you want you can borrow—" My reflection freezes and all that turns the faucet off is muscle memory.

Returning to the other side of the bed, I rest my hands on the arm rail again. The barrier gives me a false sense she's safe. "I'm back." I smile and reach inside the railing. "Your hands are cold. Let's tuck them under this blanket. Okay? How does that feel?"

My one-sided speech sounds a bit like a podcast.

"I've missed you," I say. "I've been M.I.A. lately, I—I just couldn't come back home. Don't judge me, okay?"

"Trust me, I wish you were with me. You'll love college." I pace the room, thinking maybe she can hear me better from the other side. "But—real talk—being away didn't help. I still hate our mother for what she did. And I can't forgive myself for leaving you." My head drops. "I mean, I knew you were hurting too, but you're stronger than me. And you've got your tennis team here. I'm sure Aunt Tish hovers around the house to check on you." Pulling a hair tie from my wrist, I loop my strands into a low ponytail. "The best thing I could do was stay at college." My hands fall to my hips. "Blink if you can hear me."

Blink, dammit!

"RaRa would say you're being a stubborn mule. She wouldn't be wrong either. Some would say we're a lot like our grandmother." I tap the floor with the toe of my shoe. "I know you can hear me; you just don't want to blink because I asked you to. We're not playing Simon Says, Livvy." My frustration flashes across my cheeks. "Fine, Simon says blink."

Crunching cartilage escapes each joint with a deep twist. My hands rest on my hips, and I stretch from side to side, much like a grandma doing pool aerobics.

"Taylor drives that battle box like a race car," I moan. "Tighten up, Leonard. That's what you'd say to me right now."

I wish I could hear you say it.

"I get it, you're pissed. You're the grudge champion of the year, is that what you want?" My eyes dart to hers, wondering if it's too soon for jokes, but I miss ribbing each other. Our banter is what kept me going during rough times. I counted on my little sister to hit me with a zinger, the more inappropriate, the better.

I shrug my shoulders. "My girl, I'm impressed with your commitment." Leaning over the foot of her bed, the bumpy coating presses into my palms. "Is this because I ghosted you? Cut me some slack. Oh, I am sorry I missed your birthday. Seventeen is a—or are you eighteen now?"

Admitting this position hurts worse than the others, I stretch my leg behind me, looping my foot onto the wooden chair's leg. It screeches into place. "I'll give you prom, I should have been here. It was your first one." My palm flashes to the ceiling, and I duck my head. "But Aunt Tish sent pictures after she did your hair and makeup. The salon was packed; you didn't miss another admirer."

I stare at Olivia's smooth, pale eyelids. The only thing keeping them from washing into her cheekbones is their reddened edges.

"Not that you consulted me, but the beach waves were a solid choice. And, can I just add, you rocked that dress, my girl. I mean, where did you get those curves from? When I left, you were a lanky nerd with braces. Then, you're all *that*. Shoot, sis." I raise my thumb toward the ceiling and give a two-finger jab in her direction.

I wait to see life flood her face again; Olivia Camek's not one to shy away from a compliment.

"Which reminds me, why'd you get a new dress? You could've worn any of my old ones? That green one I wore my junior year was fire too, or was it my senior year? I know they're both hanging in my old closet; our stepdad keeps everything."

I roll my eyes toward the tiled ceiling, realizing I may have to go by our family's farm while I'm here. I'm less than thrilled at the notion, but it's worth it if Liv's gown still hangs in the closet. "You wouldn't mind if I borrow that dress, would you? I've got a formal coming up. That'll look sick. I mean, it's not like you could even fit in it now. Look at you." I loop my thumb and forefinger over the sheet and around her ankle. "That dress would fall off you today." I step back, evaluate her seemingly shrinking size. "I promise I won't smoke in it. Well, that's a lie. I promise I will take it to the cleaners afterward," I say, knowing that's probably a lie, too.

A loose tube dangles from her nose. "The tape is coming off your cheek. Hold on, I saw a new roll on the counter." I leave my position, keeping her in this world with my voice thrusting over my shoulder. "The tissue is like sandpaper, by the way. Oh, I told you that already, sorry." I fumble the tape roll and decide to skip the mascara check this time. "You'll feel me touch your cheek, and yes, it's paper tape. You don't have to remind me. I know your skin is sensitive."

My mother applied cream to Liv's rashes and odd skin infections as a child. It seemed any mosquito or plant unearthed a full-blown attack on her immune system. I, on the other hand, inherited my dad's complexion. Liv was jealous of my blemish-free face and ability to skip sunscreen at the beach.

"Just don't wake up while I'm doing this. It looks important," I say. My shaking hands tap the limp paper around the soft, creamy tube keeping the same U-shaped formation.

Tan fluid running through the tube in her nose makes her skin appear even lighter. A pink-lace pattern crossing her cheekbones is the only blood flowing under her skin. "Okay, you're back together. This tube is connected to a big vanilla milkshake dangling over your head. What's this say?" I ask, reading the words *Glucerna*.

Is this like the shakes they advertise on TV? "Glu-cer-na." I try to sound it out.

I'll have to ask—no, I'll Google it before I ask her anything. How do I spell it again? The container dangles inches from my nose. G-L-U-C. Come on Google, do your thing and make me smarter than Mom.

I read: *Glucerna. A calorically dense formula that is low in carbohydrates to help minimize the blood glucose response. Specialized high-calorie nutrition for enhanced glycemic control compared to standard formulas.* Formula? Like what babies drink?

"No phones in the ICU!"

"Christ almighty woman!" I bob my phone back into my pocket. "Aunt Vy, is that necessary?"

"No phones in the ICU, Lennon. If the volume is too loud, I can show you how to adjust it."

"No, it's fine! I know you're watching me on your little monitor. Can you see the phone is no longer in my possession?" I wave my empty hands in the air for the spy camera to record.

"It needs to be off. The frequency can—"

"Goodbye."

Beep. Boop.

"She needs to go back to intimidating small children or something."

I walk to the head of Liv's bed again. "Hey, did you know you're on baby food? Is this a thing now?"

Wake up and tell me all about it, will you?

"How's it taste?"

Tell me to shut up or something.

"The baby food is not working, just saying. Hey, why are you so skinny? I mean, like, waif is so 2000s, Liv," I say, puffing my cheeks with air. "And your nails...do you dig graves in your spare time? Your fingers are scraped up to your knuckles. Why aren't you wearing our sisters' ring?" I shake my head. "I'm no athlete, but I can affirm tennis isn't a contact sport, my girl. Who hurt you?"

Can I get a head nod, a toe wiggle, or something?

"You have every reason to hate me. This is the second time I've left you behind. Once as kids, when I went to live with Dad in Florida and left you here with Mom. Then, I moved to college and didn't even call," I keep going, forcing a swallow. "It's proof I'm a selfish asshole."

My heart flutters. "I guilted you into coming to live at Dad's because I was miserable and alone. I lead you out of a perfectly normal childhood into a shitstorm of emotions. I'm a miserable human." My head hangs. "I should have encouraged you to stay with your school friends, your teammates...Mom, you, we—" Whimpering consumes my confession. "Hell, if I hadn't have moved he'd be alive today. Maybe you would be—" I pause, hoping she's not with him right now.

"After you moved, I saw how much you missed Mom. I felt worse about getting you to leave her. Every call home was to complain about how miserable we were. I never meant for anything to—" Grit crusts along my eyelids, and I blink salty water onto my cheeks again. "First, Dad's death was my fault and now, I've left you with our unstable mother." My fist slams on the bed. "Do you hear me? Dammit— this isn't how our story ends!"

A slow burn drips down the side of my nose, and I don't bother to wipe it. It falls to the crisp sheets below. Hanging my head over her bed rail, tears drip down the side of my nose and I don't bother to wipe them. I reach for speaker box controls on the side of her bed. My fingers tick the blue-and-white arrows until I'm confident no sound can register on the mic.

"Liv," I say, my eyes dart looking for other recording devices. "Has Mom hired someone to kill you, like she did Dad? Or is she doing it herself?"

My words fall apart, and I'm not sure I can finish my warning. I walk to the foot of the bed, retrieving my chair and dragging it into place, closer to her face. I squeeze a lever. *Click.* The bedrail rolls away from her mattress, and my elbows crinkle her covers.

"I'm not sure what's going on, but I'll find out and protect you. We have so much to do together: weddings to wear ugly bridesmaid dresses in, bridges to bungee jump from, fair food to gorge on. We're a team, remember? I'm the muscle and you're the heart," I say, and my voice cracks again. "I haven't always been around when you needed me, but I'm not leaving this time until Mom pays for what she's done."

CHAPTER FOUR

Olivia

Clicks and clanks tinker on my left side. A tone chimes in with the cacophony surrounding my head. I bend my brow forward and backward trying to recognize its pattern and loosen my cloaked eyelids. My lashes feather against my cheeks; a flicker of twilight streams in. Squinting, the safety of darkness returns. Troughs of rippled plastic covered in over-starched cotton guide my fingertips along their ridges. The torn skin around my thumb's cuticles grazes my hip.

I was on my way to get a manicure—

Air gusts into my lungs forcing my chest to rise, then burns a path around an egg-sized bulb lodged in my throat before exiting through my mouth. The windshear vibrates in the plastic tube resting between my teeth.

Another blast tickles my nose. I gasp. Oxygen is abundant, but the loss of control is suffocating. My eyes fling wide open. Embers crackle at every viscous layer forcing them to clamp shut again. Fluid seeps from the corner of my eye, and I'm unable to execute even the most innate reflexes. So, I succumb to the robotic rhythm again.

Humming, from my left, draws my attention nearer, easing me out of the hellish reality I'm bound to. The bars tap my eardrum, weaving into my memory. I pry one eyelid open again and a blurred shadow appears fixed to the wall. Obtrusive sunrays keep me from identifying the source of a familiar song.

Sounds evolve into syllables, then into the words. Head-to-toe tingling covers my body forcing my pinky toe to jerk. Years of harmonizing together rushes over me: at weddings, in the car, at karaoke parties, we—

My sister's with me! The singing continues and I drift into every lyric.

If this is a dream, I can't help my disappointment. I sink deeper into the scratchy bedsheet beneath me. The drugs, they...numb my mind. Inching my eyelids apart, sunlight streams over her hunched shoulder. She stretches across the windowsill and her strawberry-blonde ponytail dangles along her white sleeve. Tears inch from the corners, and my blink forces them to run along my cheeks. Lennon is home.

"'Sending love and prayers for my favorite student, my other favorite student...' that's me, 'and their loving mother.' Isn't that just the sweetest?" she asks. "Mrs. Chapman still writes in cursive? Hard to believe I can recognize her loopy lettering."

She combs through blooming mauve and blush bouquets and cheerful mylar messages tied with twirling ribbons.

"Did I have her for biology? Or maybe chem?"

She teaches chem.

"Everyone loved her. She had a way of making snarky teens tolerate science. Although, since college, my interest in polypharmacy has peaked; I doubt she'd claim her class was my inspiration."

My cheeks tighten with an exhausted smile. The corners of my lips crack, and draw my mouth away from the tube. A brief respite before returning to their fixed position.

Crash. "Shit! Dammit!" Stomping fills the silence between curse words. "Gah! I can't believe I did that." Fluid sloshes beside me. Her voice lowers. "Rest in peace little flower vase."

Lennon snorts. Sliding scuffs arise from the floor beside me before glass shatters at the bottom of, what I hope, is a trashcan. The ventilator forces a breath, I don't fight it.

"What a mess. Sorry, Sis. I'll lay these flowers on the ledge beside the others. They're beautiful. They're your favorite color." Her voice turns away. "The parking lot has filled up since we got here. Taylor's car is boxed in between lifted trucks and floral delivery vans. Speaking of…I'd better check in."

Popping bubbles fill her silence. I'm not surprised Taylor is with her. Aunt Tish must have called them. Lennon wouldn't have answered if she knew it was Mom.

"We haven't gone this long without speaking since the time they ran over my foot with the four-wheeler."

Unable to laugh at the truthfulness of her statement, I clench my jaw.

"All good." A clank lands close to my bed. "Taylor is going with Tish to find food. I'm starving. The hotel waffle didn't last long. They never do, huh?"

The smell of warm maple syrup floods my senses as if I'm a child again, bouncing on the balls of my feet in an elevator. The doors slide apart releasing the same aromas. It was Mom's visitation weekend, a.k.a. waffle weekend. Lennon and I rushed through the hotel lobby to the breakfast station still wearing our pajamas. The meal supervisor knew us by name since we stayed at the same place each trip. Our competition became an every-other-weekend ritual. The staff snuck gourmet toppings into our breakfast bar options like crushed butterscotch and whipped cream.

"I didn't see any sprinkles today." Lennon snickers.

We delighted in creating a new concoction to beat all others. Len liked hers crispy. I liked mine soft so I could fold it. The irony:

a girl who used to eat syrup sandwiches lives on a carb count these days.

"It's hard to see you like this. I mean, I know you've had sick days, but this is bad. If something else is going on, I can help you get out of it. Just because I'm not living at home doesn't mean I'm not here for you. And, before you say it, I know I haven't stayed in touch. I'm sorry."

Her speech falls distant making it difficult to decipher her mumbling. I wish I could tell her this is more than a sick day. I'm still not sure how I ended up in the hospital. And where is my car?

"I feel terrible I wasn't here to help you. Maybe your alarms were silenced or maybe the insulin was bad? If it even was insulin."

I think I know what insulin looks like.

"Odd things happen with diabetes. Sometimes it's legit, but other times it's hard to tell. If I was here, I could have looked out for you."

I'm capable of managing my own blood sugars.

It's true, there a plethora of incidents that diabetics navigate when trying to manage their glucose. Hormone levels, in a normal pancreas, fluctuate to meet the body's demands. My endocrine regulating system, on the other hand, lives outside of my body. Many combatants are out of my control: weather changes, my period, a scary movie. Virtually anything can make my blood sugar plummet or skyrocket, leaving me chasing a number back into range. A goal set by some 'white coat' in an office, who, most likely, has never experienced a high or low blood sugar event in their life. Add to that: the tubing doesn't always tuck into a hidden spot, and medical equipment isn't fashion friendly. People stare and ask about my robotic companions. Boys freak when they expect to feel a boob and grab my life saving device.

Lennon's right. This burden isn't something to wish on anyone, but I've learned how to work it to my advantage. My medical condition got us to the front of the line at every theme park growing up. I've used it to get out of two speeding tickets. And, lately, knowing the predictability of insulin response times, I've been able to manage my weight. Staying at a peak size is crucial with tennis season just around the corner. New scouts are coming to the practice courts every day. Which reminds me, I need to get back this week.

"I couldn't save Dad, but I can save you." Her crying puddles through the sheet onto my forearm.

What are you up to Lennon?

We'd lived with Dad about six months before his death. Lennon was in high school, I was in middle, and our twin half-sibs, Rilyn and Rio, were in elementary. Our youngest half-sister, Maize, was only a few months old. The pandemic moved us from an elite prep school classroom to homeschool for virtual learning, as was most of the world. 'Rona canceled Len's spring band concert and my tennis matches. Our first few months living with him were disappointing and we were still adjusting to daily life without Mom.

Our stepmom's influencer status came to a screeching halt. Peyton pretended to like the stay-at-home-mom gig, with the help of our beloved au pair, while it got her some attention with her social media following. Unfortunately, our caretaker returned to her home country before the international shut down.

Until then, Peyton's most in depth interaction with us was throwing a welcome home party on our arrival. To her VIP guest list of well-known community leaders and her closest social media followers, she was an extraordinary mother and bonus mom rivaling those of old TV sitcoms. In reality, with five children at home, it didn't take long for her to unravel.

To say my stepmother was ill-equipped is an understatement. Her idea of starting the day began with yelling at the twins to go to their rooms and not bother her with trivial problems like Wi-Fi passwords and frozen computers. My half-siblings weren't fans of sitting in front of a computer for hours. Rio cried on the daily. His freckled cheeks turned red, and he'd bury his head on his desk. Rilyn looked for any reason to be excused from class. With her mother's crystal blue eyes, and white, blonde hair, she was too beautiful to argue with. Within a few minutes of logging on her computer, her tiny feet scuttled through the house, stopping only when Peyton's voice reached her highest octave. The standoff usually ended with the mother standing at the bottom of the stairs yelling at the miniature version of herself until one, or both, of them cried. Each scream session was more epic than the last, as was my anxiety.

Living there was a stark contrast to what we were used to. When we were little, our mornings were quiet. I refused to do anything before sitting, wrapped in a blanket, with Mom for at least half an hour. Somehow, we were never late to school or felt rushed. From an early age, I was programmed for less chaos before breakfast.

Tension grew at Dad's. He worked long hours at the office and traveled frequently for his job. Lennon's grades were already in the gutter, but I refused to allow Peyton's incompetence to bring me the first "B" of my educational career. As the oldest of the brood, my sister and I teamed up to restructure our temporary homeschool schedules.

We had a good system: I ran the class work and Lennon managed meals and snacks. Peyton's idea of breakfast throwing bran flakes into a bowl, then slamming a carton of oat milk on the counter before shuffling back to bed. Lennon finally told her to sleep in; she didn't argue. I didn't push it when Lennon replaced the Oats-O-Plenty with Capn' Crunch.

Ry and Rio loved her. Not just for her frivolous food choices, but for how she connected with them on their level. She wasn't afraid to act silly or get dirty. She even wrote them a wake-up song and sung it each morning:

Good morning, good morning, let's start our day.
Good morning, good morning, let's log on this way.
It's time for our brains to wake up and learn.
It's time for our teachers to give us the grades we have earned.

My nose itches. I tense my shoulders, unable to scratch. A flare of both nostrils will have to do. Lennon may say I'm the heart of our operation, but it's really her. She loves big and sometimes trips herself up trying to help someone.

Despite our morning makeover, Peyton's outbursts were the norm. On one particular day, her crying appeared more than her daily rant. Ry and Rio were in P.E. Their jumping jacks rattled the Van Goh prints on my walls.

A few more cries rang out, alerting me this wasn't her usual dramatic episode. Running to Lennon's room, I asked, "Did you hear that?"

Lennon removed her headphones and turned down the volume of what was obviously not her instructor's lesson. "Hear what?"

"Peyton? She's crying downstairs."

"Again?" Lennon asked, pulling the earpiece back into position. "She probably broke a nail."

"No, it's bigger than that."

"Her swim instructor cancelled on her private lesson. I'm not sure how that dude is still coming to our house. Does public health not apply to swim coaches?"

A guttural groan rolled through the foyer again.

Pulling her ear forward, Lennon said, "She sounds like the chick in the black-and-white horror movie Dad likes watching with us on Halloween. The one with the shower scene."

"Is everything okay, Ms. Camek?" a stern voice called from my sister's laptop speaker.

"Yeah, Mr. Patrick. Sorry, I forgot to mute my mic, again. All is well here in the pandemic school. I'm just thrilled to be living out a historic event in real life. Man, the stories we'll tell our grandchildren—"

I pressed her laptop screen closed.

Shrugging her shoulders, she said, "He knows I'm joking. Nobody likes pandemic school."

"Consider it your first real reason to skip class," I said.

"Liv, don't let P's drama worry you."

"You know she hates it when you call her that. She's our father's wife. Show some respect."

"What? Nah. P and I are..." Lennon pounded her fist over her heart then pointed two fingers in the air before flopping onto her bed.

The moaning grew stronger. "We should find out what's going on before she scares the others. Stay upstairs," I said. "Ry and Rio are in class right now, but if they hear their mother screaming they are going to be afraid."

"Where's Maize?"

"Probably in her nursery. I'll check on her while I'm downstairs."

I followed my stepmother's sobs down the black, open-arm staircase, through the state-of-the-art kitchen she only used for Instagram backdrops, and then into Dad's office. Her slurpy inhales were a breadcrumb trail to her balled body heaving on the den floor. Her phone, face down beside her.

"Pey—, Mom?" I wasn't used to calling her by her preferred title. "Are you okay? We can hear you crying from upstairs."

There was no response to my question. I cleared my throat and asked again. "Everything alright over there?"

Her delay made me wonder if her grief-stricken state left her mute. "Well, I'll just check on Maize while I'm here, it looks like you're busy."

I turned to leave.

"Wait," she called.

I tensed watching her raise herself from the floor. Her mascara was streaked across her cheeks, her lipstick smeared into the corner of her mouth. It was not her usual hissy fit.

"Hutch...your father, my beloved husband, is dead."

Her words choked me then, much like the ball in my throat today.

It was supposed to be his last trip before a shut down on business travel. He was looking forward to spending some time at home. He'd promised to help me with my serve after school.

"He's in Boston for...work."

"Right, he had dinner with his coworkers last night." She cleared her throat. "But he didn't make his flight this morning. A housekeeper found him lying on the floor of his hotel room."

My body shook. I checked my monitor out of habit. But the blood glucose was leveling off after eating from my sister's gourmet breakfast menu. I knew that wasn't the reason for my symptoms. The news my father died pitted me lower than a hypo. It ripped my soul from my body. "I—I can't believe what I'm hearing," I said, stepping toward her.

"Don't!" Peyton leaned back on her hips. "I can't help you right now. I...I need to collect myself first. Please tell the others what's happened—"

"Me? You want *me* to tell Ry and Rio their fa...our dad is—" The word gagged my throat as sweat beaded on my upper lip.

"And your sister, yes."

"I...I need to call Mom."

"This isn't the time to be 'Mommy's little girl,'" she said. "It's time for you to grow up. I don't need sniveling children clinging to me. Have some courtesy for my grief."

I fidgeted with my device. My blood sugar waveform was sporadic much like my wrenched pulse. Standing in front of my stepmother, I was desperate to be consoled. Hopeful someone could explain why it felt like the oxygen in the room evaporated, why it hurt to breathe, or who would I become without him? Instead, she grabbed the phone from beside her soon after the words left her lips. Wiping the glass phone case with her shirt hem, she raised it to eye level. I froze watching her dab her cheeks and twist flyaway strands along her brow. With her makeup running, she started a live social media event. Dad's death was the headline.

Stumbling through the kitchen, I made my way up the stairs to Lennon's room. The walls were silent; Ry and Rio's class concluded.

"What's up?" Lennon asked, sitting Indian style on her bed. "You're pale. Is it your blood sugar?"

I shook my head no.

"Then what?"

"Dad...he's dead."

"What?"

"Don't make me say it again," I sobbed. "Peyton says he's died on his business trip. He's never coming home."

After several attempts of Lennon calling Dad's phone, each going straight to voicemail, she flung her cell across the room shattering the case like our new reality. We collapsed to the floor holding each other. It was our first glimpse at a world without our dad: one absent of his hearty laugh or his dimpled smile. A life without his strong arms wrapped around me after being defeated in a match or by this disease. In an instant, an abyss of emptiness robbed our future with him, and we were thrown into a world we'd never prepared for.

Peyton's wails filled the house again, interrupted only by deliberate answers to the streaming comments on her live feed. Maize's infant coos and giggles echoed through the foyer, and I longed to be oblivious to what surrounded me. Yet, I was forced to listen while our stepmom shares details of Dad's untimely death with complete strangers. She cried about being a young widow charged with raising the *three* children she and Hutch had together. It was the unspeakable tragedy she couldn't quit talking about.

Lennon broke the news to the twins in the upstairs loft. She was adamant to use a neutral space, so the memory didn't haunt them every time they entered the room. She handled, at least, one million elementary-aged questions about death, while I held them in my lap rocking side-to-side.

Walking downstairs, Peyton ended her online event and stretched her arms toward her children. The three of them lay on the couch together, while my sister and I slumped our way to the family room.

Lennon pulled her knees into her chest, sitting in the corner of the couch we were forbidden to use. I scanned the bookshelves for pictures of Dad desperate to remember every second, of every day, we'd spent together. Framed images showcased his beaming smile while winning awards at work, standing with MaMa Rose in front his childhood home, and on vacation with Peyton in the Turks. There was one of him as a child, close the age of my half sibs, sitting in the lap of a man wearing a matching grin, their fishing poles at the ready. One large image over the mantle framed Dad's zest for life while deep sea fishing with his boss. There was even a trio of photos: each one of my dad wearing a paper gown and surgeon's cap, holding his newborn children in the operating room. But the walls were void his other daughters. There were no pictures of me with him after our team won State or I was inducted into Beta Club. Dad wasn't standing next to Lennon after any of her music recitals or band concerts. Our memories were washed away, along with his first marriage.

Peyton returned to her DMs. Ry and Rio joined me and Lennon. I welcomed a reason to leave my unsuccessful scavenger hunt.

"Can we play Twister?" Rio asked.

I removed the white box from the cabinet and spread the multi-colored mat across the oriental rug. With a flick of the spinner, they're worlds resumed some normalcy already while I still felt suffocated.

As the twins hung in precarious positions, I left Lennon in charge and slipped down the hall to Dad and Peyton's bedroom. Closing the door, I sleuthed my way past their four-poster bed, through the sitting area, and into his closet. Button down shirts hung in order from light colors to dark high above me. Standing on my tiptoes, I yanked a suit jacket down and slid my arms inside where his once lived. The silky pleated hem of the three-button coat tickled the backs of my legs as I sat in front of his shoe cubby. With my tongue pressing the roof of my mouth, I stretched my arm inside the opening in the farthest corner, emerging with a tattered yellow and brown cigar box. It was our secret and I clutched it along with every moment he'd made me feel special.

Lennon's voice interrupted my grieving. I could tell she was talking to Mom. At first, I wanted to rush in and talk to her too, but Peyton's words rung in my head. I didn't want to seem like a baby. I remained in the closet surrounded by Dad's leathery smells until the call finished.

Entering the bedroom, I asked, "What'd she say?"

My sister jumped. "Jesus Christ," she said, placing her hand over her mouth. "What are you doing in here?"

"I could ask you the same."

"I told the kids I was checking on Maize, but I came in here to call Mom. Why are you wearing Dad's clothes?"

"I needed to feel his hug one more time," I said, my voice wobbly. "What did Mom say?"

"She said she'd be here tomorrow."

"Was she upset?"

"She sounded pretty rocked."

"I heard the doorbell ring earlier. We should get out there." I looked at my sister. "Hey Len, we're going to be okay. You hear me?"

Her fingers glided down the shoulder of our father's navy coat, and she gripped my elbow. "I know... because we are his girls."

Aunt Inez was the first of Dad's family to arrive at the house. Mama Rose didn't make the trip. It was too far for her to travel alone, and Dad's funeral was held in his hometown. I was comforted having one of his closest family members with us as our home filled with strangers.

My stomach grumbles, remembering Aunt Inez sneaking pizza past Peyton and anyone who wanted a free tour of an influencer's house. We shared a savory cheeseburger, mozzarella, and marinara combination on the black-and-white shag rug in my sister's nursery while she told us stories about her rambunctious nephew. We learned of Dad's love for frogs and fishing while dipping doughy edged crust in a buttery, garlic goo out of sight from scorned vegans.

Aunt Inez and Mom spoke on the phone. "The police said...the word is difficult for me to say aloud." She paused. "They believe Hutch's death was a suicide."

My chest ached with her recap of the investigation: death by overdose.

Lennon and I stared at each other, then she looked toward the floor. "Did you hear that?" I asked.

She shook her head no, refusing to make eye contact with me. I didn't push the discussion. My heart couldn't take anymore bombshells. Mom arrived the next day, I was numb on the trip home.

It never made sense to us. I mean, suicide? Dad? *Our* dad? Our frisbee-spinning, wheelie-popping, fishing-loving, dad *killed* himself...at work? There was no way. Hutch Camek loved *life*. He was successful at his job. His coworkers respected him. And I knew, beyond all else, he loved *us*.

Mom shared the truth when I was older. She had her reasons for letting us believe his death was self-induced, and she's made immeasurable apologies for my...our suffering. For me, having close conversations with Mom about her state of mind and, more importantly, her rehabilitation has helped me come to terms with the tragedy sooner. Lennon insists on fighting this battle alone. After she visited the jail, she shut down and refused to speak to any of the family. Even me.

I can only assume my sister is finding unhealthy ways to heal from our trauma. She's attended counseling with me and Mom, but rarely mumbles a word in our sessions. One day, I hope she can forgive our mother's fall from grace. I hope she'll stop blaming herself for leading the killer to Dad. And now, it seems she thinks she's responsible for my situation.

My heart races, unable to speak to her, knowing I am my own undoing.

CHAPTER FIVE

Lennon

Liv's mouth opens wider and the hard, plastic tube slides closer toward her chest. The ventilator signals a disapproving note. Using two fingers, I press upward on her chin, but her lips flop open with each attempt. My nostrils flare. Recoiling the white, pilled towel, I wedge it behind her left ear aligning my sister's neck and shoulders. Her demure chin draws up.

I form a boxed view of my intervention by pressing my thumbs together much like a director framing a shot. The robotic lung beside her gives silence as its approval. Stepping backwards, keeping my innovative solution in sight, the frigid countertop guides me to more scratchy washcloths stacked near the edge. I pat aimlessly behind me until I snag one from the top. There's no sign of movement from the tube. I resume phase two of my mission: ensuring her comfort.

Water cascades from the faucet over the rigid cloth. I'm mesmerized as it melts into my hand, wondering what diseased body fluid was absorbed with the last patient's use. An audacious alarm jolts me back to my task.

"The funeral took place pretty soon after his death, don't you think?" I ask, wringing the cloth. The water plops into the sink, and I walk towards her.

"Mom took us to the funeral home early," I say, dabbing her lips and forehead. "Something about allowing the family to grieve before the visitors show up." Folding a rectangle, I lay the damp rag across Liv's brow. I straighten my hunched spine before sinking into the chair beside her. Even sitting, the throbbing pain between my shoulder blades forces me into good posture.

Rilyn and Rio wore coordinating navy outfits and held Mama Rose's hands in the reception area. With deepened circles under her eyes, she held a crumpled tissue up to her face and walked in our direction.

"Well, don't you two look...sisterly today," P said, from over our shoulders. MaMa Rose daggered her with a glare, forcing P to return to lecturing some guy wearing a cheap suit and a name badge.

Leaning to our level, our grandmother said, "Your father is looking down on you both today, immensely proud of all you have accomplished, and all that's yet to come."

I peeled the edges of my fingernails with my teeth.

"What's wrong with Pey—Mom?" Olivia asked.

"I'm afraid *Peyton*..." Mama Rose cleared her throat. "Expected the Four Seasons."

I scrunched my face.

"She's not thrilled with Jack's funeral home," she said, waving her hand behind her. "But mine and Jack's families' friendship spans decades. I couldn't trust anybody else with my only child."

Tall sprays of flowers in every color lined the corridor leading to Dad's body. When I first saw him surrounded by shimmery, ivory pillows, I didn't feel the peace my mother spoke of. I tensed longing for a wave of acceptance to wash over me. It never came. Rather, saliva pooled under my tongue, and an immeasurable burn seeped from my stomach into my chest, weaving between each rib until it lodged in my throat. I could neither speak nor swallow it away.

My father's soft, sandy waves were matted across his forehead. I wanted to see his sun-touched shag scatter in the ocean breeze, but any moving air was depleted. His jaw was rigid. His eyelids, motionless. An orange paste caked around his lips, inviting my touch. Our clasped hands mirrored each other's. His because of rigor mortis, mine because I feared my impulses forcing me to fall onto his chest. Blood pounded through my vessels in by brain.

Squeezing my eyes until my skin was tight around my cheeks, I whispered, "Please God. Let Dad send me a signal to get him out of here."

I desperately wanted to race behind his long-legged stride, barely able to keep up. Tears singed the torn skin around my lips and nose. Any fleck of strength was washed away by the truth of my helplessness. His stillness proved there was nothing I could do for the man who would have done anything for me.

A tightly knotted pink and navy tie forced the rigid shirt collar under his Adam's apple. Skin folded around his neckline, making him look bigger than his real size. I'd seen Dad in suits before. He regularly wore them for work, weddings, funerals...not just his own, but his usual fit was less rigid. P should have buried him in his guayabera; the one we bought together at Coral Market. That was his favorite. Or maybe *I* felt like his favorite when he told others our story: we were on our way to see Five Finger Death Punch and I made him laugh so hard he spewed Fanta Grape.

We were close to the market. He told me whatever I picked, he'd wear it. I wanted to get him something with mangos and parrots on it, but then I knew I'd be standing next to him and there's always the off chance the lead singer would ask me to join him on stage. Dad loved the wispy linen on his chest; I loved how the sky blue highlighted his suntan. He told me it was the most comfortable shirt he'd ever worn. Throwing it on in the store, he trashed his soda-soaked shirt, and we ran the rest of the way to make the opening gig.

Nausea waved over me standing above a stuffy-ass, white prick who pretended to be Dad. I stepped away from his casket and the room spun. My hands remained forged together. Unable to unlock my knuckles, I wobbled wearing those stupid dress shoes Mom forced me to wear.

The room gasped, which served as a clapperboard for P. Cue devoted mother. "My goodness honey." She rushed toward me, as I went down on one knee. "This is all so hard on us." Her nails rubbed circles on my back as her audience gathered. Emily took pictures of the two of us kneeling together. She and P grew close during our custody hearing when Emily was supposedly represented mine and Olivia's voices in our case. She was more interested in being one of Peyton's minions.

Despite having strict instructions not to attend, Mom lingered in the reception area long enough to see me tumble. As she stepped forward, P stood beside me using my shoulder to push up from the floor.

"Ouch!"

"She's fine, Kristin," P shouted over the crowd, fanning herself. "There's no need for you to come any closer, I'll take care of her. She's just feeling a little woozy, like all of us."

The gathering crowd sighed.

"I'm okay, Mom. I just tripped," I said, wiping grit off my knees with both hands.

"Thank you for bringing Hutch's daughters. Your condolences are noted. Please sign the guest book before you go." P wiggled her bony finger in the air like a signature.

My head dropped, watching Mom turn and leave, but it was the least disruptive thing to do. She hugged Mama Rose before motioning for Tish to walk with her toward RaRa sitting in the back pew. The three leaned close, and a sneer spanned across RaRa's face as she tapped Mom's hand.

Mom bounced; Liv and I sat in the first pew with Mama Rose. Aunt Tish and Taylor positioned themselves directly behind us. Olivia was preoccupied her new insulin pump for most of the service. If I'm being honest, I was pretty freaked out about a device shoving medicine into her body, and I'm sure she was too.

A traditional Southern Baptist service took place. Mama Rose picked all of Dad's favorite hymns. Tapping the pew with her fingertips behind my head, I saw her singing through her tears. Her praise interrupted only to give a vicious glare at her newly-widowed daughter-in-law at the opposite end.

Pulling her chin tight, she said "He's with Papa Kirby, now. They've been apart since your father was a little boy." Leaning her head back, she closed her eyes toward the ceiling. "They are having peanut butter and jelly sandwiches near a honey hole, I'm certain."

During the slide show, a loud alarm rang from Liv's pump.

"What's wrong with it?" I asked.

"I don't know, I thought I silenced it," she said, pressing buttons and reading the glass screen. "There."

A few slides later, the alarm sent a three-tiered alert that jerked the congregation's heads in our direction.

"Y'all alright in the front pew?" Aunt Tish asked, peering over my shoulder.

"I feel fine. I'm not sure what's wrong with it," my sister said, tapping on the screen. Her face reddened with every reminder she'd pressed the wrong button.

Mama Rose leaned over me, and patted Liv's leg when the preacher stopped his eulogy.

"It's okay," she said, turning to face the attendees. "My granddaughter has a new diabetes pump, and we're still working out the kinks." The crowd sighed in unison. "Just another way Hutch is letting us know he's with us."

The crowd released a collective chuckle and praised my father's memory while Olivia's frustration grew. "I...I've only had one lesson on how to work it. Mom helped me set it up...I, I don't know what I'm doing wrong."

"Hey, it's okay. Nobody cares," I said. "I'm sure she's in the parking lot, we'll get her to look at it when this is over."

"Psst." I turned toward tapping on my shoulder. Handing me a wadded sweater, Taylor said, "Shove it in here."

Liv smothered the device and tucked it behind her back. With the disruption muffled, the preacher finished his sermon.

Pallbearers gathered around Dad's casket and my throat tightened seeing the preacher close the lid. Stepping behind them, I felt a strong shove from over my shoulder lurching me forward. I fell into Liv.

"Hey, watch it," she shouted.

As I was about to shout my defense, I noticed the plastic tubing connected to her stomach tightened, stretched to its farthest point. Anyone close to a diabetic is programmed to protect the insulin at all costs. Whether it's in a bag, needle, or a pump, everyone, and I mean everyone, knows the medicine is the extra baby in the room. Mom repeatedly gave us scenarios on how to manage an emergent situation, such as a pump disconnection. My sister's lifeline was stiff. A Band-Aid-like scent filled my nostrils as the clear liquid seeped around her insertion site.

In my periphery, a something clutched the black box. I clamped on to it instinctively, and followed the bony hand, up a pillowy, midnight-colored sleeve to my stepmother's icy blue stare.

"Drop the pump."

"She's making so much noise. This is supposed to be a time of peace."

Tightening my fist around hers, a guttural growl emerged. "Drop. The. Pump."

P's face wretched and the device fell from her crumpled fingers. Olivia reeled it into safety. Checking the site, and tubing, her eyes met mine and she gave an affirmative nod. But I couldn't release my grip. P's wrist shrunk in my palm until she crumbled to the ground. Every ounce of allegiance I'd pledged to her oozed into a slow-burning rage behind my sternum. Onlookers gawked as a geeky teen made a social media celebrity grovel on the tacky green carpet of a rural funeral home.

I towered over her. Drawing closer to her face, my expression remained blank. Behind P's arrogance lived the piercing fear Dad still loved Mom, loved me and Liv more than the other children, maybe even more than her. Her anxiety combatted trepidation that "likes" and comments from adorning fans were insincere or non-existent. She lived in a perpetual world of overcompensation: her mansion, money, and plastic surgery weren't enough to satisfy her. While holding her arm to her face, her insecurities flickered in her sapphire eyes while she laid at my feet like a begging dog.

My other fist reared when a firm squeeze on my shoulder turned my attention. Mom's pale pink nails rested across my black, polka-dot sleeve. I followed her arm to her eyes, and across her shoulder. RaRa stood behind her. P's hand dropped from mine, and I folded into my mother and grandmother's arms. It was the first time I'd fought to be recognized beyond my stepmother's selfishness. It was the *only* time I'd stood up for myself or my siblings. I knew Dad was proud of me for doing what he could not.

With my release, P flailed on the floor. Her thud hushed the murmuring crowd until Mom knelt beside her. Aunt Tish motioned for me and Olivia to step away. From behind Tish's safety, I, like the other onlookers, watched my mother whisper into P's ear. Then using my stepmother's shoulder as a prop, Mom pushed off of her to stand.

P's eyes widened as she shouted, "Record her. Record this woman threatening me."

Emily lit up the room with her phone camera flash, nudging her way to the front. Mom passed Dad's casket giving it a tap while shuttling us toward the exit.

From the floor, my stepmother growled, "My husband died of an insulin overdose, and his stupid kid doesn't have the decency to silence her pump alarms at his funeral."

Rumbles emerged around us, but Mom continued walking, holding Liv's hand.

"The place erupted, but Liv," I whisper, leaning over my sister's bed. "Mom. Never. Flinched."

The bedrail speaker is dark. I continue. "Everyone else was shocked to hear Hutch Camek killed himself with the same life-saving drug his daughter's life depended on," I say, pressing two fingers against my forehead. "But not Mom. She acted like she already knew."

I fling myself back into the chair, throwing my feet on the edge of the bed. "That's sociopath-level shit."

That was the first time, I suspected she had something to do with my father's death. We were told he self-injected the insulin, and that's what we believed for years. Once I was old enough to do my own research, I discovered the truth about Mom. Knowing what she's capable of, I stare at my sister lying in a hospital gown she wouldn't be caught dead in and wonder if she knows our mother is at it again.

CHAPTER SIX

Lennon

Mom told the school we were moving, and they agreed to let us finish our coursework from her house. The Coronavirus pandemic overwhelmed our teachers with policy changes; I can't say they even knew our father died. They were relieved to have two fewer students to deal with. Virtual learning was a joke. Of course, my sister made the principal's honor roll. I, on the other hand, passed along with other mercy promotions. Taylor loved having me home again. Spending seven months away from your best friend is a special form of torture.

We fell into our old routines with friends, exactly how Mom wanted. My stepdad had a big family we were close to, and they were eager to help reestablish our foundation. Aunt Audrie and Uncle Higdon gave my sister and I our first jobs at their feed and seed store. Liv and their daughter, Savannah, became inseparable. They were the same age and ran the cash register when Uncle Higdon was working with a customer. Lifting feed bags wasn't my ideal job, but Aunt Tish made Taylor help her at the salon during the summer, so it wasn't like there was anything else to do. And staying busy helped me not think about Dad.

In the fall after he died, Taylor and I did our high school thing and before I knew it, we'd our childhood felt less like a horror story and more like a good book with decent potential.

"Life felt normal again." Pulling the chair in behind me, I lean over the table toward her ear. "Trust me, Liv. I didn't want to know the truth either. I wanted to be like everyone else and accept the cover story they gave us." I lean into my chair. "But Mom's expression at the funeral...haunted me."

I scan the fluid bags hanging overhead. The beeps of the pump beside me force me to stand to read a scrolling message on the pump. *P-r-o-p-o-f-o-l.* I follow the plastic tube of milky-white liquid to the bottle dangling over our heads. It's nearly empty.

Reaching beside Liv's head, my fingers fumble along the buttons.

Beep. Boop. "Can I help you?"

"Her IV is making noises. One of her medicine bottles is almost empty."

"Okay, I'll send the nurse in."

Beep. Boop.

"Hear that, Liv? The nurse will be in shortly." Her cracked lips dangle around the tube again. I use the lip protectant from her bedside table, and layer them with the sticky balm. They tighten against my fingertip, and my heart skips.

I squeeze the handle underneath the table's edge. A firm push lowers it and I tap the brake with my toe, locking it into position beside me. A rearview check reassures me there are no eavesdroppers, I continue. "I felt guilty about Dad's death. Even after I confronted her...in jail. I was angry with myself." My hands unwind and I cradle my forehead in my fingertips. "I mean, Mom only knew Dad's business travel schedule because I blabbed it to Aunt Audrie. After your accident, she and I talked on the regular. At first, it was just a safe place to vent: I hated the beach, the heat, the obnoxious swim and tennis neighbors' kids. Then, it grew." My head lifts. "Our talks became about how I hated P treating us like her hired help: take care of the children, cook for ourselves, and be pretty-on-demand for all social media posts. I told Aunt Audrie how much we missed Dad. She knew he was on the road a lot, but she didn't understand he was working to give us a dream life." The bitten edges of my fingertips tap the bed. "Mom told us his work schedule would interfere with all the things he promised us, but we didn't listen. I was a stupid kid." My gaze darts around the room. "And I may have used your medical condition to beef up my sob story. Sorry Liv, the accident fit."

The green jagged edge of the EKG bounces along the monitor, and I feel my heart beat out of sync. My hospitalized sister's heartbeat looks like a thoroughbred's while mine is barely palpable. My brain throbs forcing me to rub my temples.

"Lennon?" a voice calls, forcing a tiny scream from my lips. "I-I didn't mean to startle you. I'm sorry."

"Vy?"

"It's just me. I need to change Olivia's sheets." She slides the door open. "The nurse will be in soon to hang a new bottle of medicine."

I can't breathe.

"You can stay and help if you want." Her plump hips waddle through the doorway, her bobbed hair shifting as she pulls the glass door and curtains closed behind her.

"Why are you closing the curtains?"

"We don't want to give the people in the unit a show, do we?" Her chuckle makes her highlighted hair fall over her round cheeks.

I want to ask her if she's here, on behalf of my mother, to kill my sister. "Are you...coloring your hair?"

I'm officially an idiot.

"You like it? Tish started last year, and we've played around with the tint. We keep getting it a little brighter with each touch-up. She says I'm too old for hot-pink hair, but I think it brings out my sassy self." Her neck wobbles her head back and forth. She removes the quilted blanket from Liv's legs. The church-windowed pattern is one I recognize from Mom's room.

She tosses the pile of sheets onto the bed at my sister's feet. "Livvy, it's Aunt Vy, baby. Don't worry, we're going to get your sheets freshened up so you can sleep tonight. We'll be gentle."

She turns to lay the quilt on the chair behind her, and I cup Olivia's IV site with my hand.

"Place your hand behind her shoulder, here."

She reaches for my wrist, and I snatch it away, exposing my sister's vein access. "Sorry, I—hospitals freak me out."

She blows a huff of air through her bangs to show her raised eyebrows. "With all the time you spent here as a kid while your mama was working, you'd think you'd be comfortable by now." Her pillowed knuckles stretch beside mine on Liv's shoulder blade. "Place your hands here, so you don't pull out anything important."

I bet you want me to pull out her breathing tube, don't you? That would make your job easier.

She stares at me. "Do I need to get someone else?"

Like Uncle Weyman?

"This may be more than you can handle."

Like my dad was?

"Lennon, I need to know you're not going to drop her. Do you want me to get the nurse to help?" she asks, nodding her head toward the woman standing by the IV pole.

"I'm fine," I growl, narrowing my eyes. My palm presses into Liv's shoulder blades, and I reposition it on a softer spot. "Okay?" I ask.

"Yep, that's good. I'll loosen the sheets over here and let you know when to pull her your way."

My back hunches forward feeling the bed raise until it taps my stomach.

"You have to preserve your back in this field. Is that a good height for you?" she asks.

How nice of you to consider my comfort, you murderer!

"With your other hand behind her hip, gently roll her onto her side. She'll face you while I tuck the sheets under her body, then we'll barrel roll her toward me."

You want to barrel roll her into a body bag, don't you?

My sister's gown slides, exposing her rigid spine through the tied slit in the back. Moving my hand to cover her, she pulls forward. Her body jerks and Vy looks at the robotic lung behind her. "Why's that machine making that noise?" I ask.

She toys with the breathing machine behind her. "Hey! What are you doing over there?"

"I'm pressing the *mute* button." Vy's eyes widen looking at the bed, and she returns to tucking sheets. "She's just coughing, but the vent doesn't like when the tube moves." She shakes her punk-rock-wannabe bangs out of her eyes.

My sister's face turns red, and she squeezes her eyes shut. Drool drains from her mouth. "She's in pain."

"We'll be done in a second. The coughing is good for her lungs, keeps pneumonia from settling in."

My sister's eyes flail open with a final thrust. "Liv? Can you see me?" I study her sunken cheeks. What have these sociopaths done to her while I've been away? Are they replacing her insulin with water? Is Mom manipulating her pump settings? No, I bet she's lying to Liv about the true carb count of those damn croissants she can't live without.

"Now roll her toward me, and pull the sheets under her," my aunt says.

I freeze.

"Y'all need a hand?" A deep voice jolts me.

"Ay!" Taylor bellows, while my eyes fix forward. Rattling a paper bag, they say, "We got some Dickie's Doughnuts for this party."

"Look who I found on the elevator." My stepdad's voice echoes against the glass. "It's my soon-to-be-famous music producer, Miss Taylor Piedmont."

"G, you know I don't identify as a girl anymore."

"Wha—uh."

"Just hug the man," Tish says. "Why's every minute with you got to be a doggone diversity lesson?"

"No shade, Moms. I'm just trying to teach sensitivity."

"Sensitivity? You just waltzed into a hospital room with a bag of doughnuts for a girl who's in a diabetic coma."

Is this my only shot at protecting my baby sister from my mother's kill plot 2.0?

"Can somebody help us?" Vy asks. "My assistant's a little green." Vy smirks, pulling the bed sheets tight under Liv's listless body.

"Sorry about that, Vy. I got distracted by all these pretty g...folks. I forgot what I came in here to do." Grey nudges me to the foot of the bed. "Can we trade places? My other stepdaughter is tiny but full of fight."

"'Lil' Bit' is as light as a feather. We don't need a lot of muscle. But we want to move quickly, so she doesn't gag on the tube any longer than she has to."

Once again, I'm a statue.

"Yeah, these greenhorns need some coaching, but they're as tough as they come." My stepdad gives a playful wink at me and returns to his duty. "Okay, kiddo, we're going to roll you on your other side. Your sis has got your backside covered. Right, *Leonard*?"

I nod, pulling the seams of Liv's gown together.

Olivia coughs, jolting her body. It's happening. Where are Vy's hands? I can't see them. Is she injecting the poison right in front of me? The gown slips from my fingertips. Aunt Tish swoops toward me to take over. I'm incapable of completing even the simplest of tasks.

"Len? You okay?"

The room comes into view as Vy tucks the final corner under the mattress. "Yeah. I'm fine. It's—just a lot to take in."

Vy straightens the accordion-like tube connected to the robot then returns to the bedside. "It is but you can do it. Let's help roll her onto her back now."

"Like this?"

"Perfect," Grey answers.

"There you go," Vy says, raising the head of the bed. Grey tucks the pillow under my sister's head, and Tish swoops in to reposition the towel by her chin again. Everyone else is taking care of her while I stand cloaked in fear. Once again, I've done nothing to protect my sister.

"Livvy, let me wipe your mouth," Grey says.

"No, I'll do that." I draw up enough courage to say. "She likes the water sponges the best."

My stepfather switches places with me along the bedside, his chocolate waves have more silver this year, too. "You're probably right about that," he says, the silver filling on his side tooth gleams at me. "You know your sister better than anyone."

"How long are you staying?" Vy asks.

"As long as she needs me."

"They have some things going on at school, but Taylor says their professors are pretty chill, right, Tay?" asks Tish.

"Moms, don't say chill."

"Is that part of your sensitivity training?"

"They know nothing is more important than family," I say, diverting Tish's scowl from Taylor's direction.

"Well, if you're here for the night, I'll get two extra sheets from the housekeeping cart," Vy says. I nod yes, looking at my friend. My heart races smelling Vy's coffee breath over my shoulder. "I'd take the recliner if I were you. The love seat pulls out, but it sleeps like a brick."

I'm paralyzed by anxiety again.

"Thanks, Vy," Grey says. "How've you been, Crumbsnatcher?"

"I'm in college now, you can't call me that," I say, only half-joking.

It's nice to be remembered as someone cute and filled with hope. His nickname reminds me of when we used to plant vegetables together each Spring. He was a proud farmer, who shared his knowledge with me and Olivia at any opportunity. Grey is innocent in all of this, that's for sure. He's just married to a heartless woman.

"I'm hitting all the wrong labels today, it seems," he says. "One thing's for sure, I'm glad to see you and Taylor. We've missed you two so much. How's college life?"

"It's cool."

"You look great, I know your mom would like—"

"I'm not staying long. The professors are flexible, but I've got exams to take. I... just came to see Liv." I turn to face him. "Do you know when's she getting out of here?"

"She should get off the ventilator tomorrow," Grey says. The deep creases around his eyes from lack of sunscreen and decades of farming stand out with his encouraging smile. "The doctors want to make sure she's strong enough to breathe on her own."

"Doctors? How many people does she have treating her?"

"Your mom could explain better—"

"That's not an option."

"I don't know all their titles. There's a doc for her blood sugar, one for her lungs, the pediatrician for the ICU, and another one for her weight loss."

"Yeah, what's up with that?" I ask, facing Liv. "Why's she so skinny?"

Shrugging his shoulders. "They're giving her liquid nutrition. It's supposed to help build her strength."

"Praise Jesus," Tish says, looking to the ceiling before digging to the bottom of the doughnut bag.

"It's been a long ride for her," he says. "For all of us."

"You got any pumpkins ready to be picked, G?" Taylor asks.

"Boy, do I?" He retrieves his hat from the table. With a flick of his fingers, he shakes his thick black curls across his neck before pulling the bill low over his brow. "The garden got away from me this year with everything we had going on. Come by the house, take a few pumpkins back to Boston with you, please." Looking at Tish, he says, "It feels like those pumpkins were bigger than them, just yesterday."

She smiles back. "Doesn't it, old friend?"

Air from the vent above cools my warm cheeks. "They'd be cute decorated in front of our dorm room."

Grey's eyes meet mine. "I'll gladly take the evening off if you two are able to stay. My back doesn't have the springs it used to."

"Good luck getting me to leave," I say.

"I'll hang out for a while too, G," Tish says, rattling the bag on the counter. Her fingers lock onto a round treat, shaking the cinnamon sugar mixture into the paper below. "I'll make sure they have everything they need before I go home."

"Thanks, Tish. Well, girls, you won't sleep a wink, but college students are probably used to that." His sun-drenched cheeks crease. "They're keeping a close eye on her blood sugar; someone is in here roughly every two hours drawing labs."

"And you steady eating doughnuts, Moms." Taylor flashes a smirk, but their mother doesn't acknowledge them. "We got this, G. You get back to the house and tend to that pumpkin patch."

"That I can do," he says, disappearing from the doorway. His tattered boots step to the nurse's station, then return to the glass door. "I almost forgot," he says. "When I heard the commotion, I laid these outside the room." His calloused hands grip a stack of photo albums I recognize. Each torn binding is a reminder of me and Olivia spreading them out on our bunk beds and looking at them together. "I thought Liv might enjoy a little walk down memory lane. Your mom says the hearing is—"

"The last thing to go," I say under my breath.

"I'm sure she'd enjoy hearing your voice rather than mine. The two of you can share a laugh about brighter days, you know," he says, handing the books to me.

My fingers rub the peeled edges of book cover and I inhale; Mom was such a memory keeper.

CHAPTER SEVEN

Lennon

Mine and my sister's achievements span across my lap in glossy shapes with playful catchphrases below: "Sisters are forever best friends", "Memory in the making", and, my personal favorite, "#blessed." Each corner is hugged by an adorable border, tying the images to a shabby chic backdrop.

Pictures of the child-versions of us shaking hands with school principals, holding our achievements across our puffed chests, and standing in contrived positions to create the illusion historic landmarks were balancing in the palm of our hands. Celebrations and memorable occasions mattered when we brimmed with innocence and hope.

Today, the dichotomy of photographing accolades while living in disappointment is evident. Where are the pictures of our anxiety or depression? Surely, Mom snapped the perfect shot of my existential crisis. All I see are fake smiles and wide laughs, just the way she wanted us to look.

"Liv, as if you aren't having a bad enough day. How 'bout we skip through our wonder years and remember how messed up our family really is?"

A strong nudge almost knocks me off my seat. "Grey left this with us to keep Liv's spirits up, Len." Taylor rolls their eyes to the ceiling. "You're a terrible nurse, for the record."

Another thing my mother does better than me.

"Let's get into it." My stomach rumbles against the doughnut I shoveled in.

"That looks like Aunt Kris. I recognize her because of her hair, but who's this dude?" Taylor squints.

My friend points to a photo of a woman wearing a cream-colored cropped tank and low-riding blue jeans. Her hair falls across her neck like autumn leaves. She's resting on the shoulder of a lanky, tanned man standing beside her. His sandy bangs ripple into a half ponytail on the back of his head. Their arms drape behind each other and their pinkies dangle from opposite beltloops.

The T-shirt Dad's wearing is one I recognize. On the front, a red-haired man stands in the center dressed as a church leader of some sort. He's wearing a sun-shaped crown, holding a scroll in one hand, and in the other, a staff with a disco ball head. Psychedelic font lines the bottom reading: *Widespread Panic Tennessee Amphitheater, Knoxville, TN March 8, 1997.* I shiver remembering how the creepy church guy frightened me as a child.

"Was Hutch a hippie?" Taylor asks.

"He had a chill side."

"Wow. I mean, I really never knew him, but to hear—"

"We only hear about his prick-side. I guess ex-wives do that to you," I say. "This must be when they lived in Kansas City. Mom told me about a blue dome like this one."

"The giant seashell?"

"Yeah, it's some sort of performance hall. She'd say, 'I can't wait to see you play in a Broadway show here.'"

"Damn! Check out that ride." My friend points to the red sports car with a scooped hood and open roof. "Hutch had game."

"I must get it from him," I say, sending us both into a rolling laugh since my awkwardness is undeniable. "Dad loved that car. Mom made him sell it after I was born."

"So, how'd they have money straight out of college? Cause I don't see a car like that in our futures."

"Dad was a few years older than Mom. He was making adult money by the time they met. He worked for a med-tech company; Mom was still in nursing school. It was her first time at a medical convention. He said he fell in love with her at his AED table because she was fascinated with the electrical system of the heart."

"Wha—"

"Geek out, right?"

"Well, it is kind of cute. He was a tall, fire-hot, fine ass—"

"Is the word you're looking for *dad*?"

"Sorry." Their head swaggers. "An established gentleman meets a wide-eyed nursing student eager to change the world one electrical shock at a time."

We both laugh. "Some fairytale, huh?" My eyes flutter, and I long for my friend's antenna-long lashes. "Complete with the tragic ending we know too well."

"Here come the stretch marks." My finger scoops beneath theirs, flipping the page forward.

A picture of Mom sitting upright in a hospital bed faces me. She's wearing a green crisscross-patterned gown. The tied neck gapes around her frail collarbone. Her cropped hair is tucked behind both ears, and her face is void of any makeup. Hallow circles overshadow her usual rich toffee eyes. With tight lips, she gives a blank stare into the camera, holding what looks like an oversized burrito.

"I'm guessing you're the lump of towels."

"It's called swaddling. They do it for newborns to help them feel comforted."

"Swaddle?"

"It's when you wrap an infant so tight, it makes them feel like they're in the womb again." Taylor stares at me. My friend is clearly shook hearing the female anatomy that rhymes with tomb. "I learned how to do it when Maize was born. When she was too young to go on outings with our nanny, I stayed home to babysit her."

"Wasn't Peyton around?"

"P was more concerned with keeping her fanbase engaged while she was on maternity leave," I say. "One day Maize was really upset. Mom video called me and walked me through the swaddle tuck. She said it saved her when I was little. Maize loved it, just like me."

"I take back what I said earlier." A nodding mound of rust-colored curls bounces in my direction. "You may be a decent nurse, after all." I smirk as Taylor turns the pages again. "Would you look at this piece of preciousness? Moms, Moms!"

Aunt Tish's eyes peel open. She rolls her neck while removing her earbud. "What, child?"

"Are you asleep?"

"I'm listening to an audiobook..." Tish runs her thumb and forefinger around the edge of her full lips stretching both corners. "With my eyes closed."

"Look at this. Here's somebody you may know."

"Spoiler alert: we're looking at Mom's scrapbook."

"Probably the one I helped her make." Aunt Tish groans, pushing up from the sofa. "Do either of y'all know how to operate a book that doesn't scroll?" Her fingers fan the air as she smirks. With her arms extended she turns the book sideways and narrows her eyes. "Mm-hmm. Your mom insisted on using that knotted wood background on the pages." Shaking her head, Tish says, "I told her then the shiplap phase was about to end. Now she's stuck with it."

"Did you go to school in Kansas City?" Taylor asks.

I shake my head no. "We moved to Birmingham after I was born."

"Babies do that," Tish says. The wheels of a wobbly legged footstool clang together as she drags it closer.

"Do what?"

Taking a carefully balanced seat, she says, "Make you want to be closer to your mother."

My friend and I scrunch our foreheads.

"It may be hard to believe now," she says, widening her eyes at us. "But it's the truth. A lot of new parents want to be close to family when they have their babies."

I shrug my shoulders. "It's odd Mom wanted to live closer to RaRa, I mean, she was the opposite of any *grandmother*."

"Lennon Rosalyn," Tish's eyebrows crease together. "Don't speak ill of the deceased."

My chest empties, and I glance at Liv lying in the bed bedside us.

"Moving closer to home put her near people she trusted and could lean on."

"So, it was all about Mom." A puff of air leaves my lips.

"It's about raising a family."

"You didn't need anyone to help you," Taylor says.

"Your granny helped me a lot when you were this age," Tish says, shaking her head. "I couldn't imagine being isolated from anyone who cares."

Staring at the photo, Dad's smile bends both cheeks. His dimples pitted. The flash flickers in his eyes. Mom's lips twist into a half smile. Her eyes are dark, hallow as she cradles me against her. It's the day of their first child's birth, and only one of them seems overjoyed. Her distance pierces me.

There was a time when I lived at Dad's house without Liv. The courts were reluctant to separate her from Mom, given her age, but I guess it was okay to divide sisters into two homes, in two different states. At his house, everyone seemed to have their place, the baby, the twins, P. When Dad was home, the two of us were inseparable. But there was always an important event or delayed plane that interfered with our time together. Most days I stayed in my room waiting for Liv to move there. Tears pool in the corner of my eyes scanning my sister's weakened body. I can't imagine my world without her again.

"After Liv was born, Hutch was really climbing the ladder at work." Her lips smack together, as she draws in close to the page. "His schedule was hectic. A lot of business travel, corporate engagements, gala events..." Fluttering her fingers in the air. "You know, the stuff you do when you want to be recognized, get the promotion." Olivia and I cried every time his car left the driveway. "Kris told me how hard it was working a twelve-hour night shift at the hospital and napping when the babies napped so she could go right back in and do it again. So, she left the hospital for a different job." Tish tilts her head toward us. "Babies do that, too. Make you change your whole damn career path, just to make sure they have everything they need." Her eyes dart between me and my friend. "She said it was hard for her to leave the bedside. Caring for patients was her gift."

"Then why'd she do it? She deserved to have promotions and fancy dinners too," Taylor says.

Tish straightens her spine and moves her head side-to-side. "She was fortunate to have a flexible career. Kris made the sacrifice and let Hutch pursue his dream. It worked out for the best. When ya'll were older, she found her way back to the bedside as a nursing instructor which was her dream job."

"Look who's in the oven, Livvy," Taylor says, pointing to Mom's obvious baby bump and tilting the album toward my sister.

Our narrator pushes forward to a section dedicated to the right of passage for every Alabamian. An infant is cuddled in Mom's arms, while she holds the hand of a toddler with feathery waves. Dad stood behind us, all of us wearing crimson and white, matching the corners of the empty stadium in the background.

"The Bryant-Denny," Tish declares, with an air of awe.

"The school our parents wanted us to go to," Taylor and I both say, sending all of us into a cackle.

Tish evaluates each picture in my family's scrapbook, acknowledging each turned page with a grunt or a hum. "My girl, Kris, looks like she needs to eat a biscuit in some of these." She shakes her head and tsks. "Here's our superstar. Liv, you were a beautiful baby."

"Len looked like a burrito," Taylor mumbles as they plop onto the sofa Tish left open.

Raising up from the edge of Liv's bed, my eyes burn staring at her. We love looking at these pictures together. Our sweet innocence, a reminder of how simple life used to be. I relax my glare and take Taylor's empty seat. "We must have formed at opposite ends of the womb," I say, noticing Taylor's wide-eyed glance at the word again.

"Y'all are alike in some ways and different in others," Tish says. "That's why the world has vanilla and chocolate ice cream. Variety is a good thing.

We giggle at a picture of Mom sitting on the ground at what appears to be an outdoor concert. I'm banging a tambourine somewhat close to her ear; Liv's sound asleep on Mom's lap.

"But you met Aunt Kris when she started dating Grey, right?" Taylor asks.

"Right. I was always close to those foolish Murphy boys. We were friends since we were teenagers. Fun fact: Grey's brother, Weyman, was my high school sweetheart."

Taylor and I make a gooey love sound like we just saw our elementary school principal kiss a teacher. "So, Uncle Wey could have been my father?"

"It fizzled like most high school romances. He was the oldest brother; a lot of responsibility fell on him at a very young age. Wey was all 'God, Country, and Family', even back then. And you know Tish needs more attention than that," she says, ending with another wide-mouthed-howl.

"So, you just hung out with his family even though you broke up?"

"We were all friends. I introduced Weyman and Vy, although sometimes I wonder what I was thinking on that one. Now we're all stuck with her," she huffs. "Higgs was a couple of years younger than Wey. He met Audrie not too long after we graduated. We all used to pick on Grey for being the runt of the Murphy litter," she says. "It's a scream now since Grey is taller than all of them."

Tish continues to talk about their glory days in high school. Sharing tidbits from stories about Uncle Higdon getting them stuck in the mud at a bonfire party they were never supposed to attend, Wey going off to join the military, and Grey leaving home to work on their family farm. All stories I've heard before at my stepfamily's events. Pointing to a photo, I say, "Here's a picture of you with Mom."

"Look at us, a couple of fine-ass mamas. We were going out to a Halloween party. She and I hit it off immediately. She's...well, you know, your mama."

"Don't remind me."

"Ah, ah, ah," she says, closing the book on her finger. Her leathery eyes glare. "I will not let you speak ill of the woman who gave you life. Are we clear?"

"Uh-huh," I mumble.

"You know I will slap the taste out of your mouth," she says, rocking the stool beneath her. "Just because you're all Ivy league now, your mama still deserves respect." Her eyes dart toward the ceiling, as she projects her voice over her shoulder. "And that goes for you too, Taylor Ragin."

"What'd I do?"

"You need to be reminded, just in case." Tish returns to the album where she left off. "Livvy, you probably laying there thinking you're grateful not to be here with this crazy crew. We just keepin' it real though."

"*Real*-real," says Taylor.

"If I've got to do story time with you fools, I need to have my own chair. Excuse me, Livvy. Your Aunt Tish is 'bout to ring somebody's bell." She stretches past us to reach the arm rail of my sister's bed.

"Can I help you?" The voice from the speaker box lights up the room.

"Bring us an extra chair, would you?"

"I'm sorry, chairs are reserved for family members only. Who's this?"

"You know damn well who it is. I—" She stops talking to whip her black and silver layers across her back, looking over her shoulder. "I can see you sitting at the desk."

"I'm busy."

"Vyantha, you're trying my patience."

"I'm hanging up now."

"Bring me a chair, woman."

Beep. Boop.

Even the screeching of Vy's voice isn't bothersome to me as my eyes fix on a picture of Dad. Coffee-hued bark covers trunks surrounding him, dwindling his athletic frame. The banks of a pond or lake blur into a late afternoon sun. His mouth is slightly open, showing his top and bottom teeth and pitting the dimples I inherited. Two wide-mouthed fish dangle from each of his hands as he showcases them toward the camera. There's a smudge of black across his cargo shorts. It's hard to tell if it's dirt or worm guts, but it's his smile that makes the shot come alive.

My mind fills with visions of him skateboarding at our local skate park. While the fear of suffering embarrassment rushed through me, the punk kids I wanted desperately to impress gave him props for having sick moves. He wore the same grin while surfing or tossing the ball with us, despite my obvious lack of coordination.

On beach days, other dads were stretched in chairs, reading books under umbrellas. Not him. He raced us to the ocean every time. His muscles flexed with each heave of my boogie board over towering waves. His cheers filled my ears over the crashing swells, casting away any fears of what lived beneath us; I sailed to the shore like a pirate capturing her bounty. That's the dad I only had fourteen years with.

I follow beaming sunrays to the center of his golden T-shirt, and fold while reading the washed-out lettering of another concert souvenir. The faded green and orange circled logo comes into view and I sink into my chair. It's the shirt he wore the day he told me he and Mom were separating. Sitting on the step together, Liv played with butterflies in the grass. Mom paced the yard, her hands on her hips, staring into the towering pines around her. He consoled me as I buried my head into *that* shirt, leaving a tear-soaked stain on the faded block lettering. He wasn't the same guy holding the two fish. His tanned skin had faded, his eyes dimmed. My hero weakened, and my world collapsed with his.

My chair screeches against the linoleum. "You good, Len?" Tish asks.

I walk to the window; the sun's reflection off car windshields forces my eyes closed. "Yeah, I'm fine." My backbone pops as I arch my chest forward. The air vent above sends a cold rush over my face, lips, and down my throat. The rhythm of machines in the room won't let me escape my reality.

"Tay-Baby, why don't you refill the water pitcher? It's on the counter." The sofa cushions creak, and the jangle of keys tells me my friend is complying. "Extra ice, I like those popcorn cubes."

The door slides shut. "It looks like another beautiful fall day, too bad we're stuck in here, right?" Tish asks. I nod, noticing the clouds form over a horizon of pine trees. "It was a brutal summer; the farmers took a hit with the drought—"

"I'm okay," I interrupt. "Those pictures made me think about Dad. I really miss him some days."

"I'm sure you do. The two of you were close. Why don't we give the album a break?"

"No, it's good for Liv. Besides, I'm sure she enjoys watching me turn into mush. She knows I avoid emotion at all costs," I say, huffing air through my nose. "That's why Liv's the heart of this 'organization.'"

"Y'all make a good team."

"Well, the 'muscle' doesn't work well, if the 'heart' is lying in a hospital bed."

"She'll be back, stronger than ever."

Despite the sun's growing intensity, I hold my position at the window. "We drove here the night Dad told us he was moving out. Mom didn't want to stay in the house in Birmingham. I was confused about how our family was going to stay together, living in two different houses. It didn't register with me that we weren't. Stupid kid."

"There's nothing stupid about the way a child processes trauma."

"Trauma? You mean like a car wreck or skateboard accident?"

"Anytime a child's world is disrupted, it's traumatic."

"Well, my parents didn't argue... in front of us, at least. I have friends who've watched their moms bleed in the living room after an argument. We didn't have any of that."

"Your mind can't tell the difference between the two, it just knows there's a total reset of what was familiar, safe. Everything the child has experienced until that point is gone."

"Maybe." I shrug.

"It's good to talk about it. Our bodies have memory. If we don't process our emotions, they can sometimes show up as an illness or pain."

My hands twist together. "I have great memories from both Mom's house and Dad's."

"Kris sacrificed a lot to make sure you maintained a close relationship with your father. For years, after their divorce, she remained committed to an every weekend schedule with him. She didn't want their issues to make you or Liv feel any less loved."

"Every weekend? No." I shake my head. "I think it was once a month or something."

"*Every* weekend." Tish leans forward. "Even when there were hundreds of miles between you." She shakes her head and smiles. "She was determined you'd have a relationship with your father. That's something she didn't have growing up."

The sun's intensity is more than I can take. A metal beaded cord passes through my fingertips, and I give it a tug, lowering the shade before stealing Taylor's spot. "Sometimes, I felt guilty for loving both parents. Mom was here. In fact, right *here*." My eyes widen and I point to the unit desk just past the sliding glass door. "And Dad... city life was for him. My heart stretched between two people, two lifestyles, two cities, but it didn't feel like Liv or I were suffering."

"Two different but both good people. They did a good job helping you find a new norm. Their efforts made it easier for their children to trust and love as adults."

"Yeah, I mean, we loved Grey and Browning when they came into our lives. I don't remember having any 'stepdad issues' like some of my friends. Liv and I loved our blended family—" My attention turns to the activity outside the room. Taylor's at the desk talking to Vy, spilling water everywhere. "Your child is making a mess again."

"What?" Tish whips her hair across her shoulders, glaring through the glass door. "That child," she grunts, stretching across the bed to the speaker. "Excuse me, Livvy."

Beep. Boop. "PICU, Vy."

"Taylor, quit sloshing that drink around out there. You're making a mess." I watch my friend's neck fling backward as Tish's instructions ring through the unit. "Get a towel and clean that up."

Beep. Boop.

"She's no server," I say, watching Taylor walk to the laundry cart.

The door slides open. Our attendant's face peers through the crack, shoving the frame with their hips. "I had it under control, Moms. No need to worry the whole dang unit. Here's your water, madame," Taylor says, using a poor French maître d accent.

"When you're finished move the container over there," I say, pointing to the corner of the room. "I know I wouldn't want to see something refreshing if I couldn't have it."

Taylor complies with my request and Tish resumes her questioning. "What about Peyton? Do you remember when you met her, Lennon?"

"She was nice, at first. But I was like four, so everyone is nice at that age," I say, tossing the paper towel into the trash basket.

"You were older than that," Tish says, pressing her finger to her lips. "I remember because Taylor went to the wedding with you. I had a time convincing your second-grade teacher to excuse the absence." Her neck sways as she pinches her lips together. "Your mom and I had the best time watching you three try on formal dresses, though. We had prom fever from that day on."

"Maybe Liv was four, then." I shake my head. Details annoy me. "We were at a trusting and likable age. Can we agree?" Tish and

Taylor nod, sipping from their Styrofoam cups. "But it wasn't long after he met P that Dad started acting weird."

"Weird, how?" asks Taylor.

"Like not-the-guy-in-the-fishing-photo weird. He was snappy on Sundays before we drove back to Mom's. Just tense, you know?"

"Well, it's a two-hour drive, maybe he dreaded it," says Taylor.

"It was more than that," I say. "On one drive home, he loaded up the backseat with construction paper, markers, and art stuff."

"Probably to keep you quiet," Taylor says.

"Sure, I mean it's understandable he didn't want us annoying him with 'are we there yet?' for the entire ride, but he was angry."

"Angry? At you?" Tish asks.

"Not sure, but he was piss—" Tish tilts her head. "He was ill about something. As soon as we got in the car, he shoved the art supplies in our laps and told us to make a sign for our room at Mom's house."

"A sign?" Taylor asked. "Like a 'Do Not Disturb' sign?"

"More like, 'Keep Out.'"

"Keep *who* out?" Tish asks.

"Browning."

"Your stepsister? I thought you said you got along." Taylor's head tilts.

"We had a lot of fun together before—" My chest sinks, and I glance at Liv's bed. "Liv and I were really young when Browning died, but we had fun memories of her growing up. She made the best blanket forts."

"What did he have against the kid? She was maybe..." Tish looks to the ceiling while tapping her fingertips together. "Nine?"

"That's what I mean. Dad started acting weird. He kept telling us 'Camek girls need to stay together.' He wanted us to exclude

Grey's daughter from everything we did," I say, feeling my cheeks warm. "To him, it was Camek versus Murphy." I shake my head hearing how odd it sounds today. "We were never allowed to talk about games we played together or things we did with our stepsister. It pressed him."

"Pressed?" Tish asks.

"Irritated." Taylor's eyes widen, and they grip the arms of the chair giving a low growl.

Their mother nods. "As a parent, that was a crass move. I mean I've never had stepchildren—"

"Or any other children." My friend inches to the edge of their chair. "When you get the best, why try for the rest?" They shrug.

Tish flashes a smirk in ther direction before continuing. "But parents shouldn't use the kids as weapons. They're all innocent." She shakes her head. "Browning was a firecracker. What'd Kris say about the sign?"

"She never saw it." I return to my seat. "The minute we asked Mom for tape her 'mom-dar' went off." My cupped hands raise in the air, shifting from side to side. "She wanted to know what Liv and I were peeling the paint off of. When we showed her, she snatched it from us."

"It sounds like your mom was trying to help you build a relationship with your stepfather and stepsister. Blended families are like slow cookers, they simmer for a long time which lets the flavors mix. A blow to the family's bonding, during that phase of your relationship, would have been quite a challenge to overcome."

The lights on the medicine pumps flicker green, yellow, green, yellow in rhythm with the wheel inching fluids into my sister's body. I wish Olivia was here to help me fill in the blanks in our childhood.

Dad's fishing picture sticks in my brain. Why can't I remember him being happy after he divorced Mom? What was he tense or sad about? The guys at work were jealous of his sales numbers and his model-quality gorgeous wife. They had twins and a plus one, all capable of being child models themselves. Dad lived in a luxurious penthouse apartment in downtown Birmingham, only to upgrade to a sprawling estate in a tropical, suburban utopia in South Florida. With each accomplishment, his misery grew.

The day he held a mini child-hate-crime session in the back of his car, his face was flushed. His eyes were red around the edges. Did Liv notice he was unraveling? Did she see him as miserable every day after?

Meanwhile, Mom seemed content returning to her hometown and living in an apartment where the cockroaches lined the building's stairs. She'd giggle at our squeals and shuttle us through to safe passage of our apartment door. Then, moving to the farm with Grey and Browning filled her with joy. I don't remember her being tired and skinny like she is in these pictures with Dad. The Mom I knew played tennis, painted beachscapes on vacation, and never missed a chance to race us from the barn. She made up games for everything: making our beds, feeding the chickens, even brushing our teeth. She, she was —well, Dad never knew that Mom. And she never spent time with the Dad I adored. They had their own opinions of each other.

Maybe, I should have asked Dad to take me fishing more.

CHAPTER EIGHT

Olivia

"It's little Livvy Lu-Lu."

I'm jolted hearing my childhood nickname.

"Now, that's the girl I remember. This is about the time I met my little princess." My foot nudged foot falls limp.

Aunt Tish's voice is unmistakable. Mumbled laughs, closer to my bed, are most likely Lennon and Taylor's. Heaving my eyelids open exhausts me. I succumb to my weakened physical state and listen to Aunt Tish describe my red, white, and blue leotard and high, gold-streaked ponytail. She's enamored with a picture of me looking over my shoulder at the photographer: my beach-tussled baby hairs delicately wrapping my brow. Wide amber eyes stare through the camera. My fellow gymnasts formed a line with me at the end. I know the exact moment they're gawking over.

The IV pump chimes fade into a roar of giant fans churning the hot, damp air in the gym. The sweet smell of insulin is replaced by a mixture of sweat and humidity.

On recommendation from our therapist, Mom enrolled us in several extracurricular activities after the divorce. All with the intent of encouraging us to meet new friends, create new routines, and put any old patterns about life with Dad in our memory folder. Mom tried to get Lennon on the 'tumble train', but she refused to do anything that oozed liquid from her pores; still does.

American flag-clad groups of tumblers tossed their petite bodies along stretches of ruby and sapphire mats. Their feet clung to the plastic with each step. Pint-sized gymnasts stepped, forward raising their hands above their heads and fixed their eyes on their destination. Stubby legs thudded into the floor. Their hands followed. And, with a slight lift from a spotter, the student's feet came together, and pride spanned from ear to ear. One after the other, they heaved themselves across the arena much like rocks flipping end over end.

I was the smallest on the team. Looking over my shoulder, the crowd stared, waiting for me to make a mistake. With my teammates waving me toward them, I obliged their invite with a wobbly somersault forward followed by a quick flick of my wrists to signify the end. We advanced to the next station.

And again, each child performed an acrobatic test. I looked at Mom sitting in the stands before executing a wimpy flop on the mat. Applause rang out, and we advanced to the next station.

In between answering my wide-eyed looks with a reassuring nod, Mom conversed with the other parents in the stands. She was home, rebuilding her life. Her happiness was palpable. "I love real people," she'd say. "Not the fake ones who only speak to me because they want an invite to the next country club brunch or charity event." These were friends of hers from college, high school, maybe longer. Mama Rose sat in the stands near RaRa able to enjoy each other's company despite their children's discord. Between fanning herself and scanning the gymnasium for a place to grab a quick smoke, RaRa released a triumphant, "Go Liv." Her cheers drew my attention away from Mom for a split second.

My teammates lined up again, this time to attempt wide-legged cartwheels with no spotter. Each gymnast followed the same pattern: arms high, a hand plant, then upright with raised arms and a smile toward the judges' table, of course. A coach motioned for me. Tensing my body, I declined his invite with a vehement ponytail shake.

Silence swept through the gym with the coach's approach. After an eye-level discussion, I planted my feet in the mat and watched my teammates move to the next obstacle. Coach left me at the cartwheel station. I watched her join the group of restless tumblers hanging like stretched monkeys from the handlebar arena.

My foot twitched inward, but I refused to show regret for my choice to stay behind. Friends waved to me from the next arena, and the coaches gave the occasional glance in my direction. All gestures made me clench my butt cheeks together and dig my tiny toes into the blue-and-red checkered mat.

A few breaths filled my lungs, then I inched my gaze over my shoulder and across the crowd until I met Mom's glare. The padded square dented deeper with my anchoring heel, and I pivoted my body around to face the bleachers. Balling my pudgy hands into fists at my side, my body became rigid, and I raised a board-straight chin to the onlookers. Mom's jaw tightened as the crowd grew restless watching the standoff between the coaches and someone's incorrigible child. RaRa stopped fanning herself and tapped my sister's knee, muffling her giggles.

"This pout on her face says it all," says Tish.

"I just wanted her to do the stunts so we could leave," Lennon says.

The tension brewed from my navel. I wanted to march off the mat, but I knew Mom would make me return. Bending my knees, my feet were cemented beneath me, binding me to the gymnasium floor. Helpless, my knees locked, and my elbows pinned to my side. My voice erupted from my throat, "I want my daddy!"

And it echoed from the center of the gym like the call of a Viking warrior. Parents looked to each other speechless, then to Mom. Budding whispers crept into the quiet crowd forming chatter about our parents' recent divorce and our abrupt move.

"Where is her father?" one man asked the audience.

All armchair counselors, their faces showed shame for this mother's wayward child.

But Mom was unmoved by my display of obstinance.

Surely, she was humiliated. Her lifetime-long friends knew Kristin Irvine was on a groveling homecoming tour after being discarded by the social elite. This was to be her re-entry into small-town society, yet her ex-husband continued to steal the show through the voice of her closest ally. While the rest of the attendees cringed, Mom's glare sliced the stagnant air straight through to my heart.

"You okay, Len?" Aunt Tish asks.

Sniffling sounds fill the room. "Yeah."

Lennon knows what I've told her. The look Mom gave me. It was the first time I truly believed she hated my father which, in turn, felt like she hated me and my sister. Mom's sinister scowl filled my memories for years afterwards, unsure of what she was capable of...until the unthinkable happened.

∗∗∗

"I'm starving," a voice says.

"Go eat, then," Lennon mumbles.

"Don't you want something? That doughnut has left the building, you know what I'm sayin'?"

My nausea subsides and I, too, want Dickie's Doughnuts.

"I'm not leaving Liv. What if she wakes up?"

My shoulders pull away from my ears, as excitement arouses spastic forehead twitches.

"The nurses said she's on medication to make her rest—"

More like, hallucinate.

"She won't wake up until they turn those off."

"She can still hear me."

Yes! Yes, I can hear you, Len. Strength returns to the pathetic hands riddled with callouses from swinging a tennis racket since I could phonetically spell the word 'Wimbledon'. The bedsheet presses against my palm.

"We'll run down the cafeteria and run right back."

"Well, y'all young things can run. Aunt Tish is gonna take it slow."

"Can you just bring me a sandwich or something from the cafeteria?" my sister asks.

"We can do that, baby, I understand. You came all this way to see her, so take your time."

Aunt Tish has a way of stretching 'baby' into four syllables.

The door slides and the voices of my childhood are replaced with the rhythm of the robots keeping me alive.

"Maybe Tish is right. Maybe you're not going to wake up until the medicine is turned down. What am I even doing expecting you to hear me?"

Lennon's hand grazes the top of the sheet, passing over my knuckles and my heart skips. My vocal cords stretch around the tube, but I can't get sound out. *I'm here. I'm awake, I can hear you.*

The bed jiggles with her forced movement and she huffs. "Dad's wedding, remember it? You were the cutest flower girl."

How could I forget? I was the main attraction.

Peyton, a Miami native living in the South, went overboard planning a Southern-themed wedding. She insisted our bridesmaid dresses resemble Scarlett O'Hara's picnic dress in *Gone with the Wind*. Lennon and I bobbled the aisle in frilly, hooped dresses with our emerald sashes draping behind.

Our stepmother's mermaid bodice embodied her twin-baby bump and flared at the bottom. It's not an outfit I recall seeing in the movie she themed her wedding after.

"Dad's, suit slapped." Pages turn. "Why were we dressed like cupcakes when P was is a supermodel?" my sister asks. "Here's Mama Rose standing behind me while the crowd sang their wedding song back to us. She looks so young."

We've looked at those pictures hundreds of times. We used to pile them on my bunk bed at night and flip through the pages making fun of each other for flat chests and failed hairstyles.

"I'll give it to P; she planned a dope-ass wedding."

She can't be serious about giving "Equestrian Barbie" credit. Our stepmom paid creative brilliance to plan the ceremony for her.

In that photo, Peyton's angled her dome of satin lace away from the camera to create the perfect profile, one hand supports her unborn children. Her chin tilts upward, as she gazes at Dad, her other hand on his chest. His mother is huddled by me and Lennon. Dad's Aunt Inez caps the group on the end.

"This little old woman," she says. Tapping fills the silence. "I remember her coming to the house when Dad died. I think she lived in Florida."

Aw, I loved the way she shuffled her feet.

"Yes, she did." A slap follows. "He used his 80-year-old aunt as one of his selling points for us to move with him. " she says. "He told us we'd still be close to family if we left Mom."

Really, Dad? We lived three hours from Disney World and that was your best pitch? I want to laugh, but this...tube...in my throat won't let me. I can't even swallow around it. My lips pinch at the corners, and I smack my mouth around the tube.

"Hey, sis. What's wrong? Why are you crying?"

More like choking.

Clunky footsteps walk away from me.

"Here," she says, her voice returning. The coarse touch of a single-ply tissue dabs seeping liquid from the corners of my eyes. Her fingers touch my face; she's biting her nails again.

"Let me get the other side."

I miss you; I miss us.

"Hey, let's try this sponge thingy." Liquid splashes beside me. "It's water. Pretend it's a Sex on the Beach."

I'm not a rule-breaker like you, Leonard. How would I know—room temperature liquid cuts through the thick paste in my mouth, and I lick every drop like it's the fruity refreshment at the bottom of a fraternity house cooler.

"You moved your tongue! Liv, you just licked this thing." Her voice slips into the distance. "Let me do the other side now."

Get me a tiny piece of that popcorn ice too, would you? I like to feel it melt in my mouth.

"Don't choke; I scooped a sliver of ice. It's the popcorn ice you and Mom—"

Mom? Did you say—I can't stop paying homage to this ice.

"Easy girl. Let's take it slow. I don't want you to get sick."

Her voice fades again, and I hear the bottom of the cup pop as it meets a surface. Screeching is followed by a loud squish, and the side of my bed dips. "Oh, you'd love this one." Her foot nudges my flimsy ankle under the sheet. "It's my birthday party. Per usual, you look jealous I'm getting all the attention. Your hair wasn't dirty blonde then; you should get highlights."

I—I'm in the hospital and you literally just dissed my hair.

She returns to humming. Paper scratches against her with her every turn. I forgive the insult, grateful to have her next to me again. She's making this hospital stay bearable.

"It's a music-themed cake. I remember that flannel shirt."

Ugh, it was never a good look.

"I loved it, but P always said it made me look like 'white trash'. I only got to wear it because Dad said it was *my* special day."

My shoulders tense remembering how our stepmother coordinated our outfits for any impromptu photo op. She'd ask her personal assistant to leave an errand for her to complete and drop the paparazzi a slight hint of when and where she'd be visible. Her favorite shot was of me and her going to the grocery store pharmacy to pick up my insulin. Leaving the store, she insisted on carrying the white bag.

On occasion, she'd notice my continuous glucose monitor. While I couldn't count on her to help me with a complicated insertion, she passed out once when I uncapped the needle, Peyton was particularly interested in showing it off to her fans. I'm sorry...spreading awareness, as she put it. My preference was to wear it on my lower abdomen, but when the device made its way to my upper body, it didn't take long for my stepmom to ask me to go on an outing. She chose my outfit, so it didn't clash with hers. Mine had to be sleeveless or cropped depending on where the meter was. She directed every move once we left the car. A picture of my DexcomTM gave her a week's worth of material to work with.

"I remember this birthday because I was..."

Scared. You were terrified to turn thirteen. Although, you were still one year below the legal age limit to choose a custodial parent, you knew—

"I knew he'd pressure me."

You told me the same, right before you spewed chocolate-vanilla ice cream cake all over the bathroom.

"And he did. He was determined to have me leave Mom."

Peyton was furious her Louis Vuitton shower curtain was ruined.

"After their wedding, father-daughter time changed. We used to go to the 'Bama games, the movies, or eat mountainous ice cream sundaes dripping with obnoxious toppings on our weekends together. Sometimes, we did all three."

Until he started his campaign against Mom.

"Then we stopped doing things that were fun and only went to quiet places, where we had 'family meetings'. I began to hate leaving the house with him for fear we'd sit for hours somewhere strategizing a plan against Mom. All he did was lecture me about opportunities I was missing by not living with him, P, and the twins.

"It was relentless. Always saying, 'Don't tell your mom,' and 'Erase this text,' or 'Let's keep this between us.' If moving in with him was such a great idea, then why couldn't I tell the person I loved the most in the world?"

Good parents don't ask children to keep secrets.

"If I told the court I wanted to move, then it automatically allowed my younger sibling to go with me. He pressured me to make the move to his house for you, if not for myself. He told me if I stayed, I was holding you back. Sometimes, being the firstborn was a real drag."

Please don't beat yourself up for this. I've made choices too.

"When Dad and P moved to Florida, I really thought he'd give up on the idea of us moving with him. Stupid kid, I guess."

You're so much smarter than you realize.

"But it got worse."

Way worse.

"Remember we had to start meeting with his neighbor, the counselor?"

What a quack.

"That one time we flew down for a weekend, and the neighbor picked us up from the airport so we could have a counseling session in the car."

Dad didn't like to waste time.

"All she really did was put our mom down and tell us how great it was to be a Florida girl."

Wack-a-doo.

"Once, I told Dad I really didn't want to leave. You know, my friends and all. Champ, our dog."

Aw, Champ.

"Dad was livid. He ranted about how much money he'd spent to get us that far, there was no backing out; I had to see it through. He knew we were a package deal."

CHAPTER NINE

Olivia

My sister took the brunt of the pressure.

For years, they prepped her for the age when she could make a legal statement: a declaration that both she and I wanted to change custody. After the ice cream cake volcano, Lennon was inducted into Dad and Peyton's legal boot camp. Every night, they drilled her about written statements to the judge, what she'd say in court, and what was shared at counselor appointments. They texted messages checking the temperature at home. It became such a routine for them that emojis were designated as quick responses when Lennon was in proximity of the "enemy". My sister received daily and sometimes hourly reminders she "wanted" to leave Mom's house for his. The twins wrote letters with elementary-school prayers scribbled inside, asking for God's hedge of protection around Len as she forged through the hell our father created.

His attack was anything but random. Dad psychoanalyzed my sister and struck her at the core of her pre-teen soul. If Lennon and Mom had a spat, he tapped into the push-and-pull at home and wove it into his campaign. An argument about a discarded flat iron became fuel for Lennon's pseudo-desire to leave home. An injustice by a middle-school teacher gave cause for her to seek a different curriculum.

She hesitated once—when he asked her to walk away from music. It's more than her passion or talent: music is my sister's limbic system. Without it, she internalizes her pain until she finds other ways to numb it. When she wavered, he promised her admission to the elite music school of Miami with a curriculum guaranteed to cater to every creative's soul. Over time, he built a staff of bass and treble clefs she couldn't resist. Len transformed from his child into his soldier.

"Here we are in front of the Lincoln Memorial." I'm grateful Lennon continues entertaining me with memories from the scrapbook. It's so much better than living in a dream fog, listening to bells and whistles beside me.

She describes our final stop before driving back home. Mom agreed to Dad's request to chaperone the school trip to Washington D.C, not knowing he was using the time to seal the deal for our custody arrangement.

"That bus ride was a nightmare. Remember the woman in the back of the bus puking the whole time?"

Yeah, it was disgusting.

"Dad pulled strings for me to go since I wasn't technically in your class."

Dad was a good salesman.

"But it was really so he could have us together, at the same time before—"

We told Mom we were moving.

"I was nauseous the whole ride home."

Dad and I played Uno at our seat while Lennon ran to the bathroom every five minutes. I laid on Dad's chest. He smelled like an old baseball glove, warm, soothing, safe. He rubbed my back and let me watch YouTube on his phone. Comforted to have him close to me, my mind raced, knowing how we were about to hurt Mom.

"Mama Rose must have taken this picture when she picked us up. It's one of all three of us looking wrecked after a week of traveling," she says. "I was numb to what was about to go down. By that time, I was in zombie mode."

There was no backing out at that point. At Mama Rose's house, her friend helped us fill out the legal forms at her dining room table. We couldn't even pronounce the words on the paper: *affidavit, custody modification, notarized*. But we signed our names to a form with our father and his mother's encouragement.

"Dad was so pissed at my letter to the judge, but I didn't know what else to write. It was something lame, 'I like coconuts. I want to be a babysitter.' I mean, that was all I could come up with." She pauses. "Not gonna lie. It was hard to pinpoint why I wanted to move from somewhere I didn't want to move from. I mean, yeah, Mom and I had arguments, but I'd lived there all my life. I had a lot of friends and was into a lot of shit at school. Why would I have wanted to leave? Life was so easy, then."

Living with Dad made it easier to see how Peyton pressured him to create the perfect world for her. He knew we were content, but his wife insisted on showing the world she was a model stepparent. She was already a medaled equestrian and local celebrity. She'd married an older businessman who spoiled her. She had twins and a newborn. Peyton needed Len and me to complete their blended family picture. Co-parenting was the only angle she hadn't used on her platform, so it fit.

"It's not like I had some burning desire to leave my room. Those posters were fire. Mom gave me total creative design."

Your room was trash, Len. I love you, but not so much your taste.

"I knew moving into the 'Barbie and Ken mansion' would be tough. Everything had to go with P's aesthetic," my sister says, through a huff of air. My guess is her bangs are in her eyes and she's too lazy to brush them sideways.

"And telling Mom was harder than I thought it would be. It was almost like she already knew what we were about to ask for. You did all the talking."

My gut wrenched asking Mom to come to the bedroom. Lennon and I sat on opposite edges of Mom's bed, while she sat in the chair in the corner of her room. My sister traced the patterns of Mom's quilt with her finger. Outlining patterns is her usual coping method when she's overwhelmed.

"So what's this all about, girls?" Mom asked. "It sounds serious."

"No, it's not serious Mama. We...Len and I just needed to tell you something," I said.

"Okay."

"If possible, can you hold your questions to the end, so I can get this out?"

Mom's lips pressed together, tightening her chin. She leaned forward, pressing her palms together on her lap. "I can do that," she said.

"Len and I...we've been planning to move to Dad's for a long time—"

"A really long time," my sister said. My eyes narrowed in her direction, and she returned to tracing patterns.

"For a while now, we've planned to move to Dad's. And we're planning to go to school there in the fall. We know it's a lot for you to hear, but we wanted to start talking about it now. So, we have time to get our things together." I paused. "You can ask questions now."

Clearing her throat Mom moved to the edge of the chair. Her knuckles were white with her grip. "I see."

"Mom, we owe it to him. You've had all this time with us, now he gets to be there for the rest of our childhood," Lennon said.

Nodding, she raised her chin and looked into my soul. "Well, I know that has to be the hardest thing you've ever said in your ten years of life." I nodded. "Because it's certainly the hardest thing I've had to hear in mine." Her voice cracked at the end.

Even if she had some awareness of what was happening, her heart broke the moment she heard it from my lips.

Our phones buzzed on the bed, but I resisted the urge to answer. I was sure it was Dad checking to see how things were going. Mom stood and motioned for us to go to the living room. She followed us down the hall. We continued to share our plans with Mom and Grey; she and Len had a heated argument. I couldn't stop crying. Mom was my best friend. I couldn't believe the words were coming out of my mouth. I'd never thought of a day we'd be apart.

As our court date drew nearer, our guardian, Emily, coached us on how to act in front of the judge. She and Peyton were good friends by that point; they had a lot in common. Both were young women from elite families with a lot of the same interests: horseback riding, social media, and shopping. Emily was assigned to serve as a neutral party to the children in a high-conflict divorce, however she befriended my stepmother during our custody modification. I'm not sure how neutral that was.

We didn't mind her visits. They were brief because she was more interested in getting into Peyton's inner circle than consulting two healthy children of wealthy parents. Their relationship benefited us in some ways. We took a lot of trips to the zoo, beach, and shopping in the premier stores of South Beach. All photo opportunities for Peyton to use in the court hearing to demonstrate how close we were to her and position her as the perfect caretaker. It took a year for the tan line around my 'Dex' to fade.

"They bought us some primo outfits for court, but we never needed them, I don't think."

No, Mom would have died before letting us in that circus. Speaking to the court was our guardian's job.

"I don't think we did. I never committed my statement to memory. Even though Dad made us rehearse it one hundred times."

Your Honor, I want to live with my father because we've lived with our mother since birth, and he deserves to have us for the rest of our childhood.

"You probably remember it word for word. You were always better are reciting bible verses and stuff like that."

If we live with our dad in Florida, we'll continue to travel to Alabama regularly during holiday weekends or school breaks. He isn't trying to keep us from her, he just wants a relationship with us. And we want one with him.

"But if I spoke to the judge, I probably would've gone off-script."

We are close with our half-siblings, we even call our stepmom 'Mom'. Nausea waves over me, and I don't think it's my illness.

"My stomach twisted closer to the court date."

It's not that we don't love our mom, it's that our dad is a good man, and we think he deserves equal time with us. In one year, my sister can decide herself which is allowed by the Alabama state law.

"He was obsessed knowing there was nothing Mom could do to stop it."

So, if you don't let us go now, we'll go next year or the next.

"It wasn't really a choice, was it?"

Your Honor, it's a simple decision for us and we hope it's easy for you too.

"We didn't speak to the judge. I know this for sure because she went off the rails," she says, with an emphatic tsk.

None of us saw the ruling coming, not even Dad. Our mother came home from court, her eyes were creased. The bags under them were hollow shells of the alert woman who left us with RaRa earlier that morning. She gave us a weak smile right before she shared the verdict.

The judge ruled for me to stay with Mom due to my age. Evidently, I was just days short of the legal limit. It was a lame attempt by the judge to slow the process down to give my sister and I time to see what was really happening. But the judge didn't know Hutch Camek. The ruling only fueled his resentment toward Mom and his campaign against her.

Len's body shuffles in the chair. "Mom jumped right in with, 'You're going to Florida, Liv stays here with me in Ellington.'"

Gut punch.

Lennon gives a long exhale. "I almost didn't go through with it."

If I knew you hesitated, I would've bailed.

"I wanted to stay."

I wanted you to stay. I wanted our lives to go back to normal.

"But I knew Dad would make my— our lives hell if I backed out. They'd committed years, and hundreds—"

Try thousands, tens of thousands.

"It *was* happening."

And it nearly killed Mom.

My sister tells me about her abrupt departure from our home. It's better I can't speak because she needs to share her perspective.

Our memories blur, especially hers. My hunch is she's never had this conversation with anybody else. Not even Taylor.

"I hated seeing Mom cry."

When we took Len to the airport on her last day, Mom was a wreck returning to the lobby after taking her to the terminal. My heart ached for losing my sister and my mother. She was never the same person after Len left.

"Baby girl?"

My sister sniffles and clears her throat. "Oh, you're back."

"Just for a minute. The unit is closing to visitors for shift change. Taylor and I need to get home."

Home? You're leaving me here with the robots?

"Moms, I'm staying with Len tonight. She needs me," Taylor says.

"I don't know if that's a good idea. The two of you here all night."

"Really? We're roommates. We live twelve hundred miles away from adult supervision. We can manage a night in a hospital alone without mischief."

"Which reminds me, that last parking ticket you received, Tay-Ray." Tish pauses, and I know she's giving her signature raised eyebrow. "That's on you."

"What? Len, tell her. That meter broke."

"The couch really sucks, Tay." My sister knows how to dodge a bullet. "Go home and sleep in your own bed. You'll be less cranky tomorrow."

"No, Liv is like my little sis too. What if she wakes up? I want to be here for it and let her know she's safe. You might freak her out."

My chest warms and I can't tell if it's my emotions or a morphine bolus.

"No cell phones in the unit!" A voice shrills from the right side of my bed.

"Jesus, be a fence," Tish says over the ringing in my ears. "Keep my crazy side within thy walls, oh Lord."

"Besides, I doubt Queen Callbox will let another person stay," my sister says.

"Taylor, if you want to stay, I'll deal with Vy. She 'bout to be wearing that speaker around her neck."

"Please. Thank you, Moms. We'll behave, I promise."

"Thanks," Lennon says under her breath. "I didn't want to be here alone. I mean, what if something goes wrong?"

Wrong? What—what is going to go wrong? Let's think positive, people.

"I got you."

"Okay, you two—"

Three. I hate feeling invisible.

"Here's my cafeteria card. I added extra money yesterday so you should have plenty. The hot grill closes at eight," Tish says, followed by two lip-smacks and one gentle kiss on my forehead.

"The snack bar is open all night. When Liv and I were in daycare, we'd get Mom's ID badge and go there at midnight."

We rolled up like queens.

"We'd get two warm turnovers and a carton of milk. I'd get the cherry and Liv loved the pineapple."

Pfft, I'm allergic to pineapple.

"I bet you thought you were big time." Tish laughs. "Well, I'm gone then. You know, I can be here in five minutes. And your mom—"

"I've got your number," my sister interrupts. I try rolling my eyes, but my eyelids are weighted down causing my lashes to flutter.

"Love you big," Tish says. "*All* of you, you hear me, Olivia Camek?"

I love you big, too. Way big. Bigger than my heart and arms can stretch. To the moon—

The door slides closed, and I hear clunking around the room again. "Did y'all get through the scrapbook?" Taylor asks.

"Yeah."

"Did she wake up?"

"Not a wink. I thought I felt her move her fingers once, but then I didn't feel it again."

My fingers shuffle under the sheets. *I'm trying.*

"Probably just her nerves," Taylor says, in a tone that makes me think she knows what she's talking about.

"Nerves? You think she's nervous?"

"I mean her real nerves, genius. You know, the ones that move her muscles. I remember when your mom used to let us dissect deer hearts at your house—"

"Gross."

Taylor's right, it was awesome.

"We'd pull the heart apart and see the vessels, tendons, and all the goop inside. Then, it would twitch—"

"And I ran inside, screaming."

Every time.

"Aunt Kris said it was the heart nerves firing, but there was no brain for them to send a message to, so there was no reaction. Maybe that's what Liv is doing right now."

Only, I'm not a dead animal. And you're no pretend surgeon with a plastic knife, cutting me open on the back of a tailgate.

"Maybe we should stick to making music," Lennon says. "Anatomy and Phys have never been my thing. That was always my little sister's bag. Maybe that stuff made her want to be a nurse."

"Or that your mom is a nurse, which could have influenced her," Taylor says.

"She'll be better than her, let's hope."

Leonard, quit it.

"Why you so hard on Aunt Kris? I mean, she is your one and only mother."

"Who killed my one and only father."

Dammit, Lennon. You know she wasn't well.

"You right, you right," says Taylor.

No, she's not right. I mean, she is, but that's not the whole story. Don't encourage her.

A chair squeaks across the floor on my right, Taylor says, "There's a lot to unpack with that scenario. I mean, it's not like you were in a good situation at your dad's. What else was she supposed to do?"

"I'm no expert, but typically killing your ex, to get your kids back, isn't the go-to solution."

"She was kind of in a tight spot."

"What is this? Defend Kristin Murphy day?" Her boots clunk by the far end of my bed, and I hear the air force out of the cushions to my left.

"Why are you so hard on her? It's been five years; hasn't she been sentenced enough?"

"Has she?"

"I think she's paid the price. She did what she had to do to get you out of a bad setup."

"Define bad setup." My sister's voice strengthens. "We had a butler, for Christ's sake."

My stomach pits listening to my sister's tenacity. She'd rather hold a grudge for the sole reason of being right than see the situation from anybody else's perspective. No matter how beautiful our lives seemed to others, we were in pain.

"Then why did you call me crying every day? Telling me how you'd made a huge mistake," Taylor says.

Lennon holds on to any quick-witted comeback, which tells me she's remembering the reality we were indoctrinated into.

"I think I'm gonna take these off now since we're staying. Doesn't the hospital still give you those 'frog feet' socks?"

Ah, the sweet sound of denial: my sister's failsafe.

"It's the truth. You remember when you first went down there? You kept telling me how it was like a cult."

"Well, cult was extreme."

"Girl, you the one that's got amnesia, not your sister—"

Excuse me! My brain works better on drugs than your two put together.

"Don't you remember that time Dad and Peyton took you to the beach and made you walk down the shoreline alone?"

My sister grunts and a wave of sweaty socks gags me.

"Each person you passed turned and said something creepy like: 'You can count on me.', 'Your mom is seven hundred miles away. You can't count on her.' Remember any of that?"

Rummaging breaks the silence. "I think Liv has socks in the hospital admission package. They usually give you a washbasin, puke bowl, and sticky socks. All essential items comatose teenagers need."

"I know you pick and choose your memories, but that's one you can't forget," Taylor says, her tone forces a response.

"Yeah, yeah. 'Your mother can't get here in time to help you.', 'Remember how far away she is?', 'We're your family now.' Those weirdos said all that."

"And then, they'd face the ocean, and, like, reeled in a shark or something," Taylor says. "Like, who's gonna argue with a shark by your feet?"

Out stepmom loved dramatic displays.

"Admit it, Len. Things were not perfect. It may have been what Aunt Kris was trying to protect you from."

The two friends fall silent.

"Dad and Peyton stood at the end of a trail of seashells," Lennon mumbles under her breath.

"What?"

Clearing her throat, Len continues. "They told me to follow the path until I reached them. It was a long way, maybe a mile or more." She grunts and I hear the boots drop to the floor. "At first, it looked like a normal beach day. People walking their dogs and playing in the sand with their kids. But then random strangers stopped me and told me creepy shit. My heart raced with every passing person. I didn't know who was programmed and who wasn't. Then I'd go a little further, thinking I was in the clear, and some freak stops fishing to say, 'We'll get Olivia here soon.'"

Ew.

"Or, 'Be sure to tell her how much better the beaches are here.', 'Don't give up on Liv.', 'Don't leave your sister behind.' It was jacked up."

Like leaving me was your idea.

"Then, I'd have to go home and help the twins write letters to Liv."

"Letters?" Taylor asks.

"Yeah, letters, notes, gifts. Anything to tell her how much we missed her. We had to use touristy postcards, the ones you see at the convenience store when you're on vacation with white beaches, vibrant umbrellas, and Hawaiian-shirt wearing flamingos. It was like were on the state welcome committee. " Lennon shuffles her socks on the floor beneath my bed. She's probably tracing the squares with her toes. "It was all P's plan to market Olivia's new home and make her put pressure on Mom to let her move. Liv was young, I can't remember how old exactly."

Eleven. You missed my birthday because Dad wouldn't let you come home until our legal case was final. He was terrified you'd get cold feet and stay.

"She was a kid, easy to manipulate. And they knew it."

You were a kid, too.

The left side of the bed dips. Her hand rests on the sheet, pressing against my knee. "I left her, and then convinced her to join me knowing all along it was a mistake. I—"

"This isn't your fault, Len."

"We should have stayed together. I missed her birthday that year. It was the first time we'd not celebrated together."

It wasn't much of a birthday. Mom and Dad argued on the phone the entire day with each other, and then with their attorneys. Dad threatened to fly to Ellington, so he could have his court-appointed time with me, but we'd planned for a sleepover party, knowing he lived so far away. Mom said if he showed up, she'd call the police. All night, I worried blue and red lights were going to wake me and my friends up.

"You're right. I had the life people make movies about, but I was miserable."

Taylor gives a self-assured huff from her chair.

"Still though. When I think about him dying in a hotel room, alone...he didn't deserve that."

No, he didn't. And Mom didn't deserve to have a mental breakdown, either. Nor does she deserve being constantly punished. They're both victims of a family legal system pitting them against each other.

"I can't argue. You had two good parents who kind of went off the rails."

"Well, life sucks and then you die."

"Is that what RaRa used to tell you?"

My body jolts laughing against this garden hose in my mouth.

"Yes."

"You need a new family motto."

Taylor wasn't wrong, but neither was RaRa. Life isn't easy and my body is slowly turning against me.

CHAPTER TEN

Olivia

Suction cup squishing fills my ears.

"The no-slip socks are no joke," my sister says. "If we want to get out of this tomb tonight, I'll need some footwear."

The bed dips. *Do not put your disgusting feet up here.*

"My Uggs are in the back of Tay-tor Tot."

I'm jostled in the bed again as Lennon lifts her foot in demonstration of her lack of planning.

"Oh, you want me to get them for you?" her roommate asks.

"Pretty please." Lennon's voice raises.

"You've got shoes right beside you. It ain't Project Runway."

Taylor has a way of keeping my sister grounded. It's good for Len. She needs something to feel normal about our lives today.

"My boots scuff everywhere I go. I can hear my mother, even now, scolding me about making more work for the environmental services team tonight."

Taylor releases a loud sigh. "Want me to get anything else?"

What kind of illegal substance have these two traveled across multiple state lines? More importantly, why am I not surprised?

If you think you're going to smoke up the bathroom in this room while my lungs are fragile—

"Nah, better not," Lennon says.

My tense shoulders release hearing my sister's moment of reason.

"Suit yourself," Taylor says. "Imma get me some while I'm down there. I need to sleep tonight."

"I hear ya. Be safe, don't let a coyote get you or something. I know you're not used to being in the country." Lennon snickers.

Taylor huffs. Our friend was the first one to show us how to jump hay bales and pick the sweetest muscadines. My mouth waters remembering the bronze- and eggplant-colored orbs dangling overhead. If it weren't for Taylor, my sister and I would have been bitten by a rattlesnake before either of us made it to our first prom.

The door slides across the metal rails and my bed dips again despite my previous warning. "Remember when we'd get these sticky socks for Christmas?"

My tongue presses against the stale paste-coated tube shoved beside my molars. Spit spills down my throat as I hear the crackling of plastic between her fingers.

"Mom stole them from the hospital, of course. They do the trick though. Definitely no *Risky Business* scene happening with these babies on."

Risky-what? The hard plastic tube shifts across the back of my throat, my chest thrusts forward tightening my airway with each jolt. My eyes clamp, tears stream from the corners. My reflexes are stunned. I can't wipe my eyes, cover my mouth, or do anything natural to comfort myself.

"Olivia?" Lennon gasps. It's okay, Liv. You're okay."

Alarms blare around me. Spasms take over my windpipe and oxygen trickles to my airway through the smallest opening. The engine in the bed grinds, pressing the mattress into my shoulder blades. Tension eases as my head leans forward. The tube shifts, but this time I'm able to swallow around the bulb. Air fills my lungs once again, and my shoulders relax, slinging my head to the side. I'm too weak to straighten it. Coarse paper dabs the corner of my eyes.

"That was a rough one. Geez, I was just saying Mom didn't always have the most thoughtful gifts. No need to be dramatic."

I'm too tired to smile at my sister's sarcasm. The bed dips again at the edge, and I know she's sitting with me. She's always wanted to be my rescuer, even when she was the one who needed saving.

I lost a brick in my foundation when she moved in with Dad. The truth was, I wasn't sure I'd ever sleep a full night again without being in the bedroom next to her. There was some disappointment for missing out on the excitement Dad promised: a new cell phone, a new baby sister, and a puppy. I felt responsible for Mom too. She dipped into an emotional abyss beyond what my sixth-grade soul could comprehend.

Lennon lived in Florida for a couple of months with Dad, Peyton, and our three half-siblings. Mom and I visited a few times. On one trip, my blood sugar plummeted. I was still new to the painstaking rollercoaster of diabetes. It was before I was deemed eligible for a continuous glucose meter by my insurance company. We relied on finger pricks to draw a microliter sample of my blood, enough for the strip to suck into the all-knowing, palm-sized monitor for a report out on how things were going on inside. Nor did I have an insulin pump to self-adjust with fluctuations. The peaks and valleys caused by food, stress, hormones, or just life were impossible to predict. The levels that someone with a normal functioning pancreas doesn't have to consider. For them, navigating insulin and glucose ratios is as natural as drawing air into their lungs which, too, is a struggle for me today apparently.

Mom said she saw me in her rearview mirror, slumping toward the window. We were jammed into three lanes of standstill traffic; she couldn't get to the emergency lane. She parked her car in the middle of the interstate to treat me. I didn't have a seizure. She said she rubbed sugary gel on my lips and gums until it absorbed, then I remember waking up hungry and confused.

Mom was nervous when she told Dad our travel was delayed by horrific traffic and my blood sugar's unfortunate decision to crap out. Most mothers would have canceled the trip, but she was determined to keep her commitment. I'd like to think the promise was to keep my and Dad's relationship from being broken by the distance between us, but at that time, the legal bombs were in full flight. I'm sure she was driven by the fear of more insults to her character, false accusations, and expensive arguments.

When I got to Dad's, Lennon was the first to appear behind the swirling, patinaed wrought iron and glass door. She flung it open, jumped the marble walkway, and charged past the tropical courtyard toward me. Planting her sneakers on the brick walkway beside mine, Lennon swept her cascading rose waves behind her shoulder before flashing a snide smirk at her baby sister. I snubbed her back. Dismissing each other's excitement felt...natural. She and Mom talked outside while I passed through the atrium to Dad's front entryway.

Inside, an abounding bouquet of metallic pastels encased a 'Welcome Home' billboard hung in the foyer. My stepmother stood under the ivory archway in a satin leopard jumpsuit, her phone held at arm's length in one hand while the other formed a flat palm. I froze watching her pull her lush, bleached strands over her bronzed shoulder as she gave a formal introduction to her live social media audience. After a blurb about her stepdaughter's arrival and a shout-out to her new Manolos, I was waved into her gourmet kitchen. A feast fit for Havana's chief of state lined the silvery-swirled countertop of an expansive island while the crystal chandeliers glittered prisms along the towering cabinetry. A gathering of the social elite and up-and-coming-entrepreneurs, all strangers to me, stood at the opposite end of an extravagant array of empanadas, pastelitos, and Cuban sandwiches.

The spanning carb count shivered me. Out of habit, I looked over my shoulder, hoping to see Mom punching the equation into her phone while looking through the glasses on the end of her nose. Instead, Lennon gave me a reassuring nod and gentle nudge on my shoulder. My tough, often emotionless, sister's lip trembled, and tears brimmed her eyes. I didn't push her for an explanation. Maybe she was excited for me to be there, or maybe, like me, she missed Mom. I prefer to think she was jealous of my face-shaped ice sculpture surrounded by fruit and assorted puddings. After all, it was an impressive display.

Rilyn and Rio danced into the kitchen and Dad soon followed. All of them shimmied their bodies to the sounds of Earth, Wind & Fire blaring through the entire first floor. It certainly wasn't that I forgot about Mom, but any worries about a failed pancreas were put on hold. Dad's house was filled with sunny smiles and bright laughter; a stark contrast to living without Lennon at home.

At Dad's, my whole body warmed, and my shoulders shook with the music around me. Lennon joined the conga line of strangers who, oddly, knew a lot about us. I shrugged off their profound interest in mine and my sister's lives and found myself stepping in rhythm with them across the marble floors. Our group passed through the living room and a den with a fireplace which I found odd for a South Florida home. Not allowing any distractions from my joy, we made a final loop through the foyer when I heard a knock from the front porch.

Mom's withered face peered through the glass entryway. She gave me a small wave and mouthed for me to get Dad. I yelled for him and scurried to take his place as the caboose. Passing him in the entryway raised goosebumps on my arms. As much as I wanted to rejoin my group, I lingered under the open arm balcony to watch my parents.

When he saw Mom at his front door, his demeanor from the "Grand Marshall of the Welcome Home Olivia" parade to a troubled soul I'd encountered on occasion. The one who encouraged us to create a "Keep Out" sign for our stepsister. The man whose brow creased while he pecked the phone keyboard. I'd scan his phone screen while he thought I was napping on his arm and see Mom's name highlighted at the top. Letters passed in tiny blue and white bubbles forming words like: 'Pathetic,' 'White trash,' and 'Disgusting.' His eyes emptied walking toward her, resurfacing a memory of him sitting across from me at a Waffle House booth just minutes before one of our many exchanges. Despite my sister telling him it was Mom's birthday, he insisted we eat together before he dropped us off. When we got to the house, all we could offer Mom was to help put away her fine china and juice-filled champagne glasses; she didn't feel like blowing out candles, although we offered.

Divorced since I was a toddler, I'd only seen them together a few times in my life. I stared at the back of Dad's pale-blue guayabera. The one he and Lennon bought at a concert. The worn edges shifted in the coastal breeze sneaking through the tiny opening he'd created to talk to Mom. My body stretched as I strained reading her lips through the coiled iron designs on the outside glass. The tattoo of his college fraternity on his forearm, raised over his head as he combed his wavy bangs across his forehead. He inched the door open. Her eyes widened as his body drew closer to hers, edging her from his home's entrance until she assumed a conditioned cower.

Dad's tone blanketed the room. "When will you realize our daughters don't want you?" he asked. "They want me. They want to live with *my* family. Olivia and Lennon want *this* life, not the sad one you have in the dusty fields of South Alabama." Mom's lip quivered. "You're holding them back by being here."

She stared at him through the closed door as he turned his back to her. My stomach pitted watching Mom's head drop. Her crimson layers draped along her pink T-shirt and her shoulders fell forward. She stepped away from the entryway, and I gripped the ebony railing to keep my shaking knees from collapsing.

Who was he to speak for Lennon and me? Life with Mom wasn't pathetic. She was the best hugger. Her flowery scent wrapped me in the bed when she cuddled with me before school. But Mom was my rock. She knew my blood sugar patterns better than I did. I'm not sure if that was because she was a nurse or a mother of a type one kid, but she'd earned the endocrinologist badge of honor.

At her house, we ate Grey's "World Famous Pancakes" and I rubbed my feet on Champ patiently waiting for my leftovers. On our days off from school, she helped us make bird food wreaths and painted canvases. We took hikes and planted gardens. We volunteered at the animal shelter and nursing homes. Mom taught us to express gratitude for the life we were granted and the people who loved us, Dad included. There was nothing that needed to change. Leaving Mom's house wasn't because we lacked anything. He'd put a romantic reel on repeat which enticed Lennon. And I needed my sister.

I resisted the urge to chase her minivan through the palm tree-lined streets of the neighborhood. Returning to my fiesta, I forced the broken images of my mother in the back of my mind.

My visit with Dad was as magical as he'd promised. He took us sailing and introduced me to surfing. While he took Lennon to the maritime museums, he arranged for me to have a private tennis lesson with a world-renowned coach. Other days, we chose between sunbathing at the VIP verandas at a nearby water park or by the country club's pool.

With every opportunity, he reminded me of the life I was missing out on. He'd say, "You and your sister can be together if your mother would just sign the papers." It sickened me to hear him talk about it like she was re-homing her pets.

When Mom returned, Lennon and I spent a couple of days in her hotel room. I pretended not to hear her crying next to me in bed. On our last day together, she took us to the beach, although we both knew Mom hated it. Pale-skinned, Irish women have a long-standing love-hate relationship with sand and surf. We didn't tell her that Dad took us earlier in the week. She acted weird, but I assumed she was worried about us being eaten by sharks.

I took a break from practicing my new surfing skills and she made me check my blood sugar. Kneeling beside her, she wrapped a towel around my shoulders and said, "If you want to live here, with your dad and sister, you can stay."

As much as I wanted to be reunited with Lennon, I didn't want to leave Mom. My heart ached to hear her say she and Grey bought the house next door and she'd still tuck me in at night. But I knew the perfect world didn't exist for my sister or me. Our entire lives, we'd been trained to accept this or that, here or there, her or him. This was no different.

Saying no to Dad's offer meant disappointing my hero. I didn't want to bring more tension between him and Mom so, I agreed to continue with his plan. But he failed to teach us how to manage the guilt that came with watching our mother succumb to his repeated blows. There was nothing mentioned about how the luxuries at his house were afforded by his relentless commitment to long hours at the office and weekly business travel. Dad didn't account for how his two daughters would fit in with a stepmother who wouldn't come close to filling Mom's role in our lives. Dad drifted after the paperwork was signed, and my sister and I wandered in a lost vat of emotions with our greatest ally a state away.

Tears pool in the corner of my eyes as I question why the two most important people in our lives hated each other. We loved both homes, and both our parents, but we were forced to exclude one to have the other. I hope Lennon doesn't try to dry my crying with more sandpaper.

"When you moved to Dads, I thought that would fix everything," my sister says, from the end of my bed. "But it just made me feel more guilty. I knew how close you were to Mom. You were so young, too. I...I needed to convince myself I didn't make a mistake asking you to move there. Halloween was supposed to seal the deal."

Full-size candy bars from South Florida's top 1%.

"But it rained."

More like monsooned.

"Our first trick-or-treat at Dad's house was a wash-out, so he dressed up like Freddy Krueger to cheer us up."

He really tried.

"I think he knew we missed trick-or-treating with our friends at home. Even though we would have worn homemade outfits, it was our tradition."

My friends missed an Eeyore from their group. I still have the ears.

"Then Maize was born, and we were both so excited to have a baby sister. But we weren't allowed to do anything with her in her nursery. It was used for photoshoots."

A permanent Instagram backdrop.

"I don't know if I told you, but that snow globe Mom gave Maize when she was born...I saw it in the trash."

Peyton would never have allowed something she'd deem tacky.

"We thought we were gaining a new family, but we were really part of P's brand campaign of being a devoted mom and stepmom."

The other holidays weren't much better.

"Remember the vegan thanksgiving?" My bed shakes with my sister's amusement. "What happened to the sugary sweets we had at your homecoming?"

She didn't need to entice us once he had Mom's signature.

"There were none of our favorite meals. No Mama Rose's 'Sweet Potato Shuffle' or RaRa's "Famous Rolls.""

You know RaRa bought those at the Piggly Wiggly, right?

It was hard to convince us brussels sprouts covered in cashew cheese were as delectable as macaroni with Velveeta. On Mom's next visit, she, to no surprise, showed up with a cooler filled with our holiday favorites. Most of her money went toward travel and lodging, so we didn't do a lot away from the hotel grounds. We spent our time with her making crafts or playing gin rummy and eating our favorite homemade meals.

"She always came up with something stupid to do. Remember we'd spent one day at the hotel making care packages for homeless people?"

Those gift bags were fun to make. My messages were uplifting and esteem building, I like to think.

"Mom, when she visited, she looked—"

Sick.

"Like she did in some of those pictures with Dad. Her hair was stringy. Her cheeks, less plump. She looked tired."

Miserable. Empty.

The door slides across the metal tracks. "Here." A thud lands on my bed. "Put something over those bark skinners, would ya?"

"Thanks," Lennon says, reaching over my leg to retrieve the apparel Taylor's thrown her way.

"Why's Liv sitting up? Dear Lord, did you try to feed her?"

"No, I'm not an idiot. She was coughing; I raised her bed."

"Well, she's not coughing now," Taylor says. "Lay her back down so she can rest." The faint smell of burnt leaves and jasmine draws nearer and I feel the bed recline. "There, that's probably better, my girl. What y'all yapping about?"

"About when she moved to Florida and our first few months living with Dad."

"Do you think that's a good idea?"

"It's not like she can pick the topic."

Smartass.

"You don't want to upset her. I mean, what she survived was worse than your beach walk through Crazy Town."

And I thought cashew cheese was the worst that could happen.

CHAPTER ELEVEN

Olivia

My stepmother's interior designer was on speed dial.

The decorating team spent three days at Dad's house creating a winter wonderland in the foyer dedicating one full day to erect a twenty-foot tree in the center. Snow-flocked branches adhered to cotton-candy metallic, basketballs dripped in iced lights while coordinating ornaments dazzled, covering each square inch of the tree. Peyton said she went with a pink theme because it was Maize's first Christmas, but we all knew she was copying her archenemy, Kylie Jenner.

Guests were greeted by a grove of evergreen-wrapped walls and mellow tones of joyful tunes playing overhead. Peyton avoided using the traditional red velvet and fluffy, white-edged tree skirts. Her trees were anchored by ornate gingerbread houses fully decorated with peppermint candies and gumdrops and train stations with working engines. After twisting the last sprig into symmetrical patterns along the double staircase banisters, the crew worked for two days outside wrapping the courtyard's palm trees with the same motif.

"My alarms went off once or twice," my sister says.

She was the only person at Dad's house who followed my blood sugar readings on their phone. It was an app my dad and Peyton told my endocrinologist they downloaded and monitored, but that was a lie. Once I moved to Dad's, it was comforting knowing somebody else in the house was watching out for me. Lennon didn't know what to do about my lows or highs, but it made her feel good to point out I sucked at pretending to be a functioning human.

"I must have gone back to sleep."

Same.

"I wish you'd knocked on my door. I had a stash of sugars hidden from P."

Any stockpile Lennon claims to have stored was likely for her own enjoyment, but it's nice to know she would have shared.

Peyton had a zero-tolerance policy about sugar in our house. When I moved in, Dad and I shopped for my favorite low snacks to create an emergency supply, ones with quick response times. He explained to his wife Type 1 diabetics can drop low and there's a medical need for sugar. But she couldn't grasp how high fiber fruit wouldn't work as fast as a Smartie. My stepmom refused to store a candy haul in the kitchen where Rilyn and Rio could find it.

Dad grabbed the Whole Foods bag from the kitchen island, and I followed him through their bedroom and sitting area, to his dressing suite. I got lost staring at the paneled shoe cubbies lining the wall until he knelt on the beige carpet beside me. His waves bounced reaching behind a tattered pair of Birkenstock sandals in the far corner. Returning from his excavation, he held a mustard-colored box with the words "San Cristobal" written in gold. He flipped the latch and said, "Olivia Rose. Let's put your treats in here with mine." The beaming light from above captured the gold flecks in his eyes, reminding me where I'd inherited mine. He stacked the cigars on one side, and I packed the space with Smarties, Lifesavers, and, his personal favorite, sour apple Jolly Ranchers. "This is just for me and you."

With a final blare, I woke up to the room drifting around me. I peeled my eyes open to focus on the monitor flashing red numbers:

50, double arrows down. Heaving my body onto its side, the cold tile on my palms indicated I'd misjudged the distance to the edge. On my hands and knees, I followed the reflection of Christmas décor to the upstairs landing past my siblings' bedrooms. I glanced at my monitor hoping the first alert was a compression low from laying on device. The red letters screamed: LOW.

Calling for help would have been a smarter option. But in a drunken hypoglycemic stupor, I was more worried revealing our special treat box would get him in trouble. At the top of the rounded stairwell, I pushed up from the floor and steadied myself on the banister. The chandelier spun. My knees buckled. The metal railing slipped out of reach, leaving my fingertips tangled in a faux pine garland. Plastic hooks popped open with each tumble. Ribbons of décor fell to the floor beneath me. One strand formed a loop and dangled toward the marble until it lassoed the center tree.

"The crash woke everybody up."

I don't remember any of this.

"All I saw was the tree stretched from the stairs to the front door. Crushed pink glass scattered everywhere. I thought there had been an earthquake."

That was your go-to emergency, in Florida?

"Then, you were crumpled in a ball at the bottom of the stairs. Garland wrapped around your wrist; your feet laid on top of one of the gingerbread houses. I ran down the steps. When I got to you, you were sweaty, pale. Your lips smacked..." Lennon gives a loud inhale, then releases it. "I froze. I mean, Mom handled any close calls at home, not me.

"By then, Ry and Rio were screaming from the landing. Peyton shot out of her room with her night mask around her forehead. When she saw the tree, she fell to her knees and started screaming."

She was as emotionally stable as a folding table.

"I shouted at Rio to call 9-1-1.He ran to the upstairs home monitoring system and pressed the red cross on the panel. An operator answered within seconds over the intercom. I gave him the address and told him to ask for an ambulance. They told us to try giving you anything with sugar in it, but they didn't know P very well." My sister snickers. "Ry and Rio stayed with you. I hurdled the river of broken glass to get to the kitchen and snagged some honey from P's tea caddy." My bed wobbles with my sister's repositioning. "The operator said emergency responders were on the way, but you couldn't wait for them. She said your brain was starving, so I rubbed your lips and gums with the honey. Ry got the glucagon case from the medicine cabinet under our bathroom sink." Air forces through her nostrils. "If the honey didn't work, I—"

It's frightening to hear my life balanced in the hands of my befuddled sister and two first graders. Every year, Mom hosted an educational session on how to save me in times such as this one. It's the unwritten agreement all T1s have with their family and friends. It's not something we choose. Trust me, it sucks being a burden. I'm sure Len wished she'd paid more attention.

"Rio, smart kid, by the way, pulled up YouTube on his tablet. I spelled the name of the medicine, and he found a one-minute tutorial within a few clicks," she says. The bed shifts with her motions. "I pulled off the cap, stabbed the little bottle-thingy, and gave it a firm push, mixing the powder with the fluid. Then, I sucked it back up in the needle-thingy."

All these years she's lived with a diabetic and she still can't remember the medical terms. I know I was given this curse because I'm the stronger one. If Lennon was the T1, she'd live in denial until her death. No—no, she wouldn't die because I'm a responsible caretaker. I would have *listened* to the family emergency training.

"I was just about to jab your butt—"

My butt?

There are a plethora of muscles where glucagon can be absorbed, but my sister's ADHD didn't get her to that part of the one-minute video.

"And the EMTs showed up." Her hands clap on her leg and the bed shakes again. "You moved your head a little, then opened your eyes. I was shaking so bad, the needle dropped, shattering the vial.

"P joined us in the foyer, holding Maize on her hip and wearing a fresh face of makeup." Lennon huffs. "She never missed an opportunity to see a fan." The bed shimmies again. My mind follows the popping sounds of her movement around the room. "She turned on the waterworks for the ambulance drivers. She said she was frightened for her daughter's safety and all that, but they stayed focused on you."

I always knew how to steal the spotlight from Peyton.

"I'm pretty sure I threw up on the paramedic who was helping you."

Shocker.

"It pressed her when they wouldn't let her sign the permission to treat you because she wasn't a legal guardian. The stepparent doesn't have the same rights as the parent, I don't think. Dad was out of town."

He was never home.

"I offered to call Mom, but P nudged the crew onto the front porch and closed the door." The sound of her popping her knuckles distracts me. "When she returned, the four of us were sitting at the bottom of the stairs, covered in candy wrappers from Dad's and your secret stash. At least we weren't smoking his cigars." Her laugh spans the room.

Too scared to go back to my room that night, Lennon swept glass from a small area in the foyer where we camped out. She made a pallet from living room blankets and throw pillows we were never normally allowed to sit on. Then, she raided the kitchen and piled snacks all around us like a fortress. We watched old sitcoms on Ry's tablet until we couldn't stay awake. It was something Mom would have done.

"I called Dad first thing in the morning. He told me I did the right thing by calling 9-1-1. He kept telling me how sorry he was, and that he was on the next flight home."

I'm sure it scared him.

"But he also told me, under no circumstances..."

...could Mom know.

Mom and Dad were finalizing the paperwork on the new custody arrangement. He knew if Mom heard about my accident, she'd back out of the agreement. None of us wanted the fighting to return.

For the few weeks I'd lived with Dad, there was peace. Mom remained committed to giving us the space, she said, we deserved. There were no more argumentative phone calls during all hours of the day. Dad's perpetual state of irritation ended. Peyton wasn't nagging him about how much they were traveling to Alabama or taking time away from her social media events to consult attorneys. Although I missed Mom, it felt like our family was moving forward. So, I agreed to keep our secret until the final papers were approved by the judge.

But none of us knew Mom's low glucose alerts rang through like I was still in the bedroom across the hall.

***

Why'd Hutch care if Aunt Kris knew about his Christmas tree crashing in the foyer of his mansion? Sounds like karma to me." Taylor snorts.

"Welcome back to the conversation, Tay. And I thought my sister was the only one in a coma."

"Whatever." Taylor stretches their words through a yawn. "Five a.m. came early. My eyes got heavy listening to your walk down memory lane. Now, I'm starving."

A nap followed by the munchies, how original.

"I was just sharing Liv's wrecking ball act for Christmas."

"Oh yeah, she was always stealing the attention somehow." They laugh.

"Then we went to Mom's for our winter break and had to keep it all a secret. Liv made up some bullshit story about the bruises on her legs, but I don't think Mom bought it."

"Moms usually see through our BS. Maybe she wasn't worried knowing you were with Liv through whatever it was. I mean, that's one of the reasons she agreed to let her live with him in the first place."

"No, Mom knows Liv got a scumbag of a sibling."

"If Liv was here right now, you know what she'd say," asked Taylor. "Stop blaming yourself, Leonard."

My sister huffs air through her nose, my nickname for her still triggers her.

"I don't blame myself—"

"That's cap." Taylor tsks.

"Facts. Olivia wouldn't be in this mess if I hadn't moved to Florida in the first place. You can't argue with that."

"What I'm arguing is that you live your life like a goddamn fool because you think somehow you don't deserve to be here."

"I—like to have a good time."

"Standing on the balcony beam of the dorm was hella fun, wasn't it? You got us evicted."

"We needed to move. I was tired of those idiots."

"Why do you insist on living out a death wish? Do you think you could have stopped Liv from falling down those steps that night? Do you think you could have prevented her from getting diabetes? Do you think you could have stopped your dad's death?"

"I don't know, maybe," she mumbles. "Not the diabetes thing."

"Do you think you could have kept your little sister out of the hospital?"

"Possibly."

If you only knew why I'm here. My thoughts hurt me more than any needle ever has.

"If I stood up to Dad in the first place, none of this would be happening. Mom wouldn't have become deeply depressed, he'd still be alive, and my sister would be celebrating her senior year, not lying lifeless in a hospital." A loud, mucous-filled sniffle follows.

"Why do I act like this?" she asks, before blowing her nose. "Because doing scary shit makes me feel alive again, like I did as a kid. For a minute, when the endorphins hit, I forget I'm the lazy sister who did nothing when Liv needed me the most."

"You shouldn't have been asked to choose one life or the other. That's too much pressure on a kid."

Lennon's voice softens. "And I'm older than her. I should have known better."

You were thirteen.

"Oh, excuse me." There's a thud on the linoleum, followed by the sound of dragging chair legs. "Olivia was into Barbie dolls, so we know she was incapable of choosing a custodial parent. But for you, an emo-loving, flute-playing, mediocre middle schooler, life-altering decisions flowed naturally."

"Those were dark years," Lennon says. Laughter erupts and I wish I could join them. The two friends take a minute to regroup their conversation.

"Are you ever going to give yourself a break?" our friend asks, gentleness flowing from their lips.

"My life is a break. I'm not the one in a hospital bed."

"She doesn't blame you for her illness."

"No, but I've added stress to her life which makes it worse."

"How?"

"By being an idiot. Being weak. Not giving her a better role model to follow."

"How?" Taylor's voice strengthens. The chimes of the ventilator keep rhythm in Taylor's silence.

"By getting our father killed. Don't you get it?" Lennon's voice drifts toward my left again, and her shuffles are softer this time. "I'm the one that cracked when we went home for Christmas. We were supposed to keep Liv's accident a secret. I didn't tell Mom, but I started talking to Aunt Audrie. The night before we flew back to Dad's, I told her everything. About the beach intervention groups,

Liv's fall, and how miserable I was there. I even told her Dad and P were planning to adopt me and Olivia."

"Why would you make that up?"

"Because I knew it would piss Mom off."

"Your situation was miserable. Liv's life was in danger. You did the right thing. You never should have been asked to keep a secret from your mom."

"I told you, I'm an idiot. I guess I wanted them to be angry at Dad and P, so they wouldn't blame me."

"Nobody blamed you for moving, Len. It was a court order."

"The truth was: I loved Dad, but I wasn't happy living with him. Hearing P was cutting Mom out infuriated Audrie. She was a foster kid, so she knew what that meant."

No legal rights, no custodial rights, no interaction with us…at all.

"Aunt Audrie ran back to Mom, which is what I wanted, but I never meant for her to kill him." My sister sobs, muffling her cries with her hands and I hear Taylor's feet shuffle over to her. "Mom never would have known if I'd have kept my mouth shut."

My body aches hearing Lennon hold onto this guilt. She doesn't realize Mom received a critical low alert on her phone the night of my accident. When we were home for Christmas, Mom asked me about it. She told me how helpless she felt watching my blood sugar plummet, then go flat, then spike again. The waveform from my Dexcom™ showed her the events of the night. The next day, she verified with her insurance company, the emergency teams were called to the house. While terrified to go against Dad's commands, it was even harder for me to lie to Mom, face to face.

It was me. I told her everything: the fall, how shitty Peyton was to us, how Dad was always gone, and how every minute we regretted leaving her. It was me!

My heart races again. I've got to get off this ventilator.

Mom wasn't surprised to hear how Peyton was acting towards us. At the hearing, our judge had no idea how much Dad was traveling. Mom said he hid his real schedule, so it looked like he was home every evening. We were both becoming a whipping post for Peyton's anger and resentment toward Mom.

She tried to do the right thing by keeping me and my sister together, but it took a toll on her mental health. When we visited her for Christmas, her clothes sagged over her skeleton arms. Her collarbones stuck out. The corners of her lips were covered in broken skin. Later, she confessed she'd returned to bingeing and purging. She said it was less about her appearance and more about having control over something. And, now, I know what she means.

"Who knew you were a damn bodybuilder? Holding on to all that dead weight," Taylor says.

"Whose fault is it then? If it's not mine? Is it Aunt Vy's? Is it Aunt Audrie's?" Her tone firms. "Or was it Aunt Tish's fault?"

"My mother didn't have anything to do with your dad's death and you know it," Taylor says, their breathing slowing down. "It's fine with me if you want to live your life believing you got him whacked, I really don't care. Just quit dragging me around in your sob story."

"Fine," my sister says. Their voices separate.

Lennon, I told Mom everything. She heard it from me!

Alarms blare beside me. "What's happening?" asks Lennon, but I don't stop. My arms quiver like I'm dredging an anvil from the depths of the ocean floor. My fingers grip around the tube at my lips.

"Her hand. It's on the breathing tube!" Lennon shouts. The bed leans to the right, and I feel her reach over me for the intercom. "Hey, hey! We need a nurse."

"Olivia, stop!" Taylor's voice shouts from the left, and my eyes open. Light daggers through my squinted lids, and I recognize their rusty, tinted coils as bouncing in front of my face. Their freckled cheeks are close to mine.

"We need help in here, now!" Lennon says to the speaker box, followed by a stampede of clogged feet entering from the right corner of the room.

"Get the arm restraints," someone shouts.

"No, don't tie her down! She's not an animal," my sister says. "We can hold her until you get her comfortable again. Taylor, grab her other hand."

Taylor secures my wrist and pleads, "Miss Thing, you don't want to do this."

Let me do this, I can breathe. Lennon needs to know the truth.

"Liv, I know you can hear me," my sister's voice echoes, each syllable ringing longer than the last.

The problem is you can't...hear...me.

"Your lungs are still weak. You need this robot. I'm sure you're scared, but I'm here with you, and I'm not leaving. Let me worry about things out here, while you get stronger."

"Olivia, you're at the hospital still. Don't be afraid, your friend and sister are here with you. You should start to feel more comfortable very soon."

"Why are the skinny bitches always so strong? I don't know how much longer I can keep her down. Is someone giving her something to put her back to sleep?" Taylor asks. Their voice strains. Their palms sweat meshing with mine on my arm.

"Her IV site is clean, ready for injection. Two milligrams of morphine in," a strange voice says. "Someone, record the time, please."

A fog blankets my eyes again. Images flutter through my mind: me and Lennon playing fetch with Champ, my younger self dancing under freshly washed sheets while Mom hangs them on the clothesline, our mother reading to me and Lennon in the bathtub as toddlers. One eyelid peels open. The light stings, but I glimpse a flash of my sister's pale rose waves draped across her face. They tickle my chin, as she tucks them behind her ear. Tears brim the reddened edges of her fern and timber eyes. She looks so much like Mom. My heart aches remembering how much I miss them both.

Her face comes into my narrowed view. She mouths words, but I'm deafened by the fog blanketing my senses. My body warms, and people's voices sound like their underwater. Relaxing my grip on the tube, my arm slides to my side. I just hope Lennon doesn't do anything stupid before I can tell her what she needs to hear.

CHAPTER TWELVE

Lennon

"Any idea what she was upset about?" asks the nurse.

Liv's wrist goes limp in my hand. I release my grip and softly stretch her fingers onto the sheet before slipping away in silence.

"We were just talking to her, and...and she woke up," says Taylor.

"Her eyes opened. She's listening to us. She wanted to say something," I say. My lip quivers and I tuck it in between my teeth. If I know my sister, she wants to tell me what a piece of shit I am and I should leave.

"The morphine will keep her comfortable, but if she's combative again, we'll have to restrain her," the nurse says, widening her eyes.

"I don't think that'll be necessary. We're here for the night. If she gets restless, we'll call for help," I say, nodding my head in the direction of the speaker box.

"It's good when family can be at the bedside. The patients do much better."

"When do you think she'll get off of this thing?" I ask.

The nurse tilts her head sideways and pulls her chin tight. "If she can rest tonight, it will help her strength tomorrow. A pediatric intensivist will see her in the morning. They should write orders to extubate if her blood gases look good."

"Extu—"

"We're music majors." Taylor's comment prompts a smile from the nurse as if she already knows we're starving artists.

"Extubate. Remove the breathing tube, but her blood gas has to be stable."

"Her blood *sugar,* you mean?" I ask.

"Her glucose is stable. We're giving her insulin and checking the levels every two hours. The blood *gases* show how much oxygen she's getting. If her oxygen level is good, then we'll know she's ready to breathe without the machine. The respiratory therapists draw blood around four o'clock in the morning, so the results are in by the time the docs get here."

"Good thing I didn't want to sleep tonight," says Taylor.

The nurse laughs. "Being a devoted family member is a hard gig. She's lucky to have you."

Taylor follows the clinician to the door and looks over their shoulder. "I'm going to step out for a few. That...that was a lot."

The remainder of my ponytail falls over my shoulder with my nod, and the door slides across the steel track behind Taylor. Tracing the wires streaming in and out of Liv's peaceful body, my heart rate slows to a normal rhythm. The emergency lights on the ventilator are dark, and the alarms are silent. Machines churn and hum again in sequence.

On the wall, my options for lighting are dim or off. I flip the switch, but the room still seems bright given the main unit is still in full functioning mode. A parking lot filled with streetlamps gleams, prompting me to shuffle to the window and adjust the louvers.

The room darkens and I step sideways toward the sink rubbing my temples in the mirror. Twisting my face side-to-side, I notice my forehead sweat has cooled into a sticky film along my hairline. I close my eyes, and rest my palms on the steel countertop beneath me. What am I doing here? I'm not sure if I'm helping or hurting things.

The sharps container on the corner comes into view as I reenter our reality. I lean closer. A glass vial balances on the lip of the plastic door. The label reads: *Morphine Sulfate Injection 4 mg/ml.* Four milligrams? The nurse said she only gave two. Plucking the tiny glass bottle from its precarious spot, I save it from plunging onto the broken glass and exposed needles below. With two fingers, I grip the fractured neck and swirl the clear fluid collected at the bottom. Hands pat against the glass door, and I give a sideways glance at the tattered edges of my friend's Vans peering beneath the curtain. Swiftly, I snag a square of gauze from the supply counter and wrap the vial's broken edge before sliding it beneath my skirt's waistband into a small inner pocket. Then, I hurry to Liv's bedside chair.

"Oh, we're doing this again?" Taylor asks.

My shoulders tense. I glance at the sharps box, it looks untouched, then back to Taylor. "Doing what?" I ask.

My friend tilts their head toward my lap at the album resting beneath my hands. "Uh, yeah." I open the book to a random starting point and hold it in the light casting in from the nurse's station. "It's better for her to hear happy memories than me and you arguing."

Taylor leans over me, pointing at a picture of me wearing a long white gown, with a slit up to my mid-thigh. "What was happening here?"

"A midlife crisis."

"Looks more like a high school dance."

"And it was on Valentine's Day. My first answer stands."

"I remember this weekend," Taylor says, waving their finger in the air. "Aunt Kris and Moms planned a trip around your dance. We were supposed to celebrate your achievement in the Magic

City." Taylor shimmies their shoulders, walking toward the recliner. "She rented a house on the beach for the weekend and everything." Shaking their head. "The three of us ate at this fancy seaside place while you...danced or whatever you call those odd body movements." Snorting, Taylor continues, "I was just along for the free vacay."

"Whatever. You know you missed my ass." We both laugh, and the edge of the ampule ticks my stomach, forcing me to run my thumb along my waistband to reposition it.

Taylor's eyes raise. "You alright over there? You look like you're in pain."

"All good. This skirt wasn't made for long days and doughnuts. I adjust my body in the chair. "We messaged every day on Insta, even after I moved."

"I know, you're needy like that," Taylor says, and we both laugh. My stomach relaxes against my waistband again, testing the gauze shield. "Moms took her tackle box of makeup and hair supplies. Your mom brought four dresses she'd found at Dillard's. She was so nervous about you not liking one, but then, you know..."

My body sinks remembering the exhaustion I felt after a week of being P's show pony. Every day after school, she dragged me to a different dress shop across the greater Miami area. I explained, multiple times, I wanted to wear something simple, comfortable. A shift dress with spaghetti straps, low-heeled strappy sandals. She didn't care. This was her golden opportunity to use me as a rags-to-riches moment for her Insta nation.

It was Mom's visitation weekend, and I kind of wanted her help. I didn't have a lot of style, but I didn't want to overdo it either. Mom knew the vibe I was shooting for, but P didn't include Mom, or me, in any decisions.

The former "Miss Miami Beach," was on a quest to relive her glory days. Mom's minivan and Dillard's dresses would have scarred my stepmother's image, so they were simply excluded from the equation. It was easier for P to appear the perfect parent by pretending Mom didn't want to, or couldn't afford to, be the guardian I needed.

The picture was the last day of Hell Week. I didn't go to school because P wanted me to have everything done before my mother arrived. At the house, her glam squad took over her marbled bathroom. I was shoved into a high-back chair while brushes prickled over my cheeks, eyes, and lips. They yanked my hair through a flatiron. My collarbone tingles recalling one stylist grazed it with her inferno tool. The final result: a sleek low bun so tight the corners of my eyes slanted.

"She treated me like one of her beauty pageant apprentices."

"You looked like you were working a corner," says my best friend.

My lips thin, and I narrow my eyes, but I can't argue. I felt my IQ drop as low as my neckline.

"Our mothers chattered the whole way to Hutch's house, like giggly schoolgirls. Then, when we drove into the subdivision, you were already taking pictures in front of the waterfall." Taylor's fingers motion an air-pinch. "Silence."

A lump lodged in my throat seeing Mom's minivan round the corner of the neighborhood entryway. Her face went blank, and Tish threw her hands over her mouth. I shucked the urge to break away from the photo session and grab them both. Mom had no idea how much I hated being forced into living like someone else, but we had this teenage game we played. The one where the teenager does everything to prove she's nothing like her mother, and Mom plays along.

"Kris cried the entire time we were at dinner," Taylor says. "That was low, even for Peyton. I mean, there was enough room for two moms to help out."

That wasn't part of P's social media blast though. She was pushing for a blended family affiliate.

As soon as the photo sesh ended, my stepmother was nowhere to be found. She didn't care my crush showed up with another girl at the dance. It wasn't P bandaging my feet from the heels she insisted on me wearing. She wasn't interested in my style, my vision, or my goals. And she sure as hell didn't care about my relationship with my mother. The only thing that mattered to Peyton Camek was the likes and follows on her profile.

"This must have been the next day. Here we are at the beach."

Taylor points to a picture of the two if us in matching red, white, and blue bathing suits. Our sandy arms wrapped around each other's shoulders. Our eyes squinted from the sun reflecting off the white sands. The emerald waves swelling behind us.

"The waves crashed our boogie boards pretty hard," Taylor says. "Livvy, look at you playing volleyball with the boys. You little tomboy."

The ventilator chimes for Liv's response.

"We thought we were all that, didn't we? Ha! It was crazy to be on the beach in winter," they say, shifting their weight into the other hip behind me. I glance again at the sharps container, then back to the book. "The Camek girls actually looked like they had color during them days. " Taylor laughs.

"That's a spray tan. P made me get it for the dance."

My perfectly hued friend snares her glowing green eyes in my direction. "White folk are wack."

"It was worth cold paint slapping me in the face. Can you imagine me in that white gown if I hadn't? I'd look...translucent."

I tug the bottom edge of my shirt, and my finger touches a wet spot. My breath goes stale.

Taylor walks to the sofa while joking about my family's lack of melanin. She slices me with a stare.

"What?" I ask, my trembling fingers follow my shirt's hemline to a squishy section of fabric.

"Nothing," they say, falling into the cushions bumping the back against the wall.

"Liv, I need you to help me out here," I say. "Not all of us have model-quality skin genes."

"White teeth. Full lips, go on, go on."

"Yeah, all that. Those damn eyes," I say, leaning into my friend's ego. I pull my finger from under my shirt. A tiny dot of my blood pools on the pad. I press it against the inside of my shirt and straighten my back.

"My daddy has sexy eyes. My mama's got sexy lips. It's hard to be my friend. Don't hate."

Taylor boasts as I slip my index and middle fingers under my waistband to locate the source of blood. The fabric of my skirts absorbs the liquid as I press into the wound.

"What's your deal over there? You look like you're sitting on needles."

Readjusting my hand on the book again, I say, "Those eyes messed me up at the Fourth of July party."

Taylor scans me, head to toe, from the edge of the bed with an arched eyebrow. "You should have minded your own business,

Lennon Camek." My friend raises their chin and slides a chair up to the bed's corner. "Nobody asked you to be a detective that day."

"You must have amnesia. You said, and I quote, 'Let's be Law and Order S.V.U. division,' that morning when I texted you what was going down."

"I was perfectly fine helping you solve your own family mystery. Who asked you to help solve mine?"

She's right. Originally, we were supposed to solve Dad's death, but I lost focus. Aunt Vy and Uncle Weyman threw a huge Fourth of July barbeque every year, still do. Since they lived across the street from my best friend, I never minded attending family events.

"Those American flag bikinis made an appearance again."

"Those were boss." Taylor lays their head back on the cushion, twisting to remove a tube of lip balm from a front pocket. They dab, then smack their lips together. "We bought them at the store and couldn't wait to be twins."

***

It started as the most enjoyable day I'd had in months since Dad died. Liv and I struggled despite regular counseling. The Murphy family tradition brought some normalcy back to our routine though. For as long as I could remember, we joined Grey, his brothers, their wives, and his parents for a barbeque celebration. There was a buffet of grilled foods: hot dogs, hamburgers, and chicken bursting with smoked seasoning. Liv and I enjoyed exhausting ourselves playing swimming games with cousins before enjoying a bowl of Aunt Audrie's famous homemade peach ice cream in front of an impressive firework show. Grey's dad, Ches, went all out every year. We'd even had the police show up for a few obnoxious displays.

At my house, Taylor and I finished our fourth video chat confirming our matching bathing suits were indeed cute when I noticed RaRa and a crowd of Murphies huddled around on the front porch. Mom's crimson locks blanketed her lap. The onlookers spoke to the crown of her head while her face was buried in her hands. Aunt Audrie fidgeted with her coal-colored mermaid-braid, taking an occasional glance through the blinds. I tucked myself behind the door, keeping Mom in view.

RaRa's hands flailed in the air, which was her usual storytelling method. Her eyes widened with her overenunciated syllables. She glanced to the others on the porch who chimed in between her bangles shifting back and forth. Grey rubbed Mom's back, and Ches stood with his arms crossed in the corner until Mom finally reared her head.

A child knows their parents' tone from a single glare. It's the body language also known as "the look." Her eyes...reddened, her teeth clenched, and her brow furrowed. The two women argued for a while longer. It was obvious RaRa had overstepped, again, and Mom was worried about the aftermath. At first, I thought maybe RaRa had ordered pizza for my band camp, which got her in trouble with the healthy-lunch police once before. But it was bigger than that.

Mom slammed her fist on the table in front of RaRa and shouted, "I was fighting."

To which RaRa responded, "You were losing."

Mom fell silent and leaned into her seat.

RaRa was never pleased with Mom's decision to agree to Dad's demands and let Olivia join me. She wasn't one to hide her emotions about the topic either. RaRa smoked a cigarette while, Aunt Audrie leaned toward Mom with clasped hands. Mom didn't acknowledge them. Much like her look at the funeral, when P advised the toxicology report showed a high concentration of insulin in Dad's body, Mom never startled or gasped at any of the revelations my family shared on the porch. She listened, narrowing her eyes. Then nodded with a smirk that confirmed my suspicions: she'd started formulating her alibi.

Olivia darted out of her room. "Like my coconuts?" she asked, shaking her shoulders as the leaves of her grass skirt swished.

I stumbled over Champ who was eager to go outside. "Uh, yeah, Livvy. That's cute for a pool party, but it's not a luau."

"I know this already, Leonard," she said, placing her hands on her hip. "I just like it."

She walked toward the porch to let Champ out, and I scrambled down the hall to my room. Catching my breath, I did what any teenage girl would do: I recruited my best friend to help me expose my mom as Dad's killer.

"What was I thinking agreeing to your half-cocked plan? I mean, did she even say the words, 'I killed Hutch Camek'?"

"Not the words but the look. We've discussed this before."

"Well, if her look convinced you she was the murderer, why didn't you bust her on the porch?"

My eyes dart to the fading person beside me. Her face is hardly visible behind the shadows. "My little sister tried to impress me with her coconut bra."

"Livvy, you hear that?" Taylor asks. "I bet you still rock that hula outfit, sis."

"I lost my train of thought," I say, biting my lip. "Then I rode to the party, sandwiched between a little Moana and the killer."

Taylor closes their eyes and shakes their head. "What a sight when we got our gang together. Two American flags and one hula dancer, 'bout to throw hands at our family's annual pool party."

"Olivia didn't know anything was about to go down. Her chest was out because she was in love with her coconut bra." We both laugh, turning to our silent companion.

"What were you actually going to try to pull off at the party?"

"I planned to push Mom in the pool..." My face flushes, hearing how ridiculous it all sounds now. "And drown her."

"Lord have mercy on you and your family's absurd way of managing stress." Their palms press together and raise to the ceiling. "Can we revisit this for a minute?" I follow the edge of the ceiling tile with my eyes, listening to Taylor reassess my strategy. "You was gonna push your mama in the pool, then jump on her to keep her underwater? All ninety-eight pounds of your scrawny behind."

"You were supposed to help me."

"You gotta a big heart," Taylor tsked. "That's why I love you after all these years. You know I'm your ride-or-die, but I will not get this hair wet. That goes for tonight too if your outlandish plan has water involved."

"Well, it didn't go down. You sabotaged it," I say, jutting my chin and closing the book in my lap.

"Me?" Taylor leans over their knees and places their hand on their chest. "How did I mess up your family drama?"

"Those eyes," I say, widening mine, knowing they're marbles compared to her gems.

"My *eyes* foiled your plans to drown Aunt Kris?"

"B-because..." I stammer. If Taylor approaches me, this bottle will drop from its precarious position under my waistband. "It...was during COVID. You...you were wearing a mask." My friend pinches their lips together, laying both cheeks into their palms. "Everybody's eyes jumped out because of the masks. I couldn't help but see the resemblance with my stepdad's."

"They sexy, I know." Taylor leans back again, crossing both arms across their chest and extending each leg. Their shoes rock sideways on the heels. "My eyes are my superpower."

I exhale slowly. "Thinking Grey and Tish had an affair...rattled me. I forgot the vengeance I was there for."

"You stomped onto that pool deck. Social distancing be damned." Taylor laughs and leans toward Olivia. "Remember when your hot-headed sister did that, Moana?"

My sister's chest rises with the machine pressure. "Maybe I wasn't hot-headed. Maybe I was excited to have another sister," I say, raising both eyebrows in my friend's direction.

"I'm only four months older than you, fool. Besides, you've seen my mama. Does she look white to you?"

"Half-sisters, then." I shrug. "I thought Aunt Tish and Grey had a baby together."

"I should slap you for her."

A smile creeps across my face. "I ran around to all of the Murphy men, staring at their eyes over their masks. Grey, Uncle Higgs, Uncle Wey. I even went to Miss Twila to see if I could see her eyes—"

"A regular Nancy-damn-Drew."

My head shakes. "Her eyes didn't jump out like the others because she refused to wear a mask. Then I went to Mom."

"You asked your intended victim if her best friend had an affair with your stepdad?"

"No! I asked her if she'd noticed how much your eyes looked like the Murphy's."

"And how'd that work out for you?"

"She blew it off. Just said we'd talk about it later." I give a one-shoulder nudge and pull lint from my non-slip socks, wincing as I sandwich the cut between my stomach and waistband

"Kris wasn't gonna rat on Tish. That'd be like me ratting on *you*. Did you actually think you was going to get somewhere with her?"

"I don't know what I was thinking. I mean, my best plan, that day, was to drown my mother at a family cookout. We can agree my rational thinking was skewed."

My friend concedes with a nod. "You're welcome; my eyes stopped you from making a disastrous situation worse. You wouldn't have lasted one day in juvey."

Drowning my mother would have made me feel better in the short term, but what would it have helped? I'd have two dead parents instead of one. My sister and I'd be orphaned. It wasn't a good plan; I concur. As much as my friend likes to think their family tree is what saved me, Taylor was there for the real showstopper.

CHAPTER THIRTEEN

Lennon

After interrogating my family's varying shades of hazel irises, I took a break from my quest to identify Taylor's bio-dad. I scanned the crowd for my next person of interest, shielded behind Mom and Aunt Tish.

RaRa greeted our group. Her bangles clanged together on her wrist keeping time with the taps from her matching high heels. Her candy-apple red fingernails pinched a cinnamon drop which I accepted. Drawing nearer to the adults, she lifted her chin, shifting her lightening-white bangs across her forehead. Her signature emerald gems peered over her patriotic face-covering toward Mom.

"I'm owed a credit," she hissed.

With her gaze locked on her daughter's, RaRa's aged hands cradled a palm-sized black device. Aunt Tish swept it away, tucking it into the front pocket of her red-and-white striped linen shorts. My paper mask clung to the sweat dripping from my nose and lips. Hot, recycled oxygen filled my mouth.

A passing cloud dimmed the scouring sun long enough for my eyes to focus on the unsuspecting partygoers, each wearing festive outfits for the holiday celebration. The men adjusted their visors, wiping sweat from their brow, while the women dabbed napkins over their lips. The splash from a poorly gauged cannonballer sprinkled my foot and ankle. But I continued evaluating if anyone saw my grandmother's contraband.

Ches leaned on the worn-wooden gate with his arms stretched behind him while smoking a cigarette. His calloused fingers flicked the fiery ash before he tucked the smoldering butt in his pocket as two uniformed men approached. My stepgrandad offered the men a welcoming handshake and he returned to his relaxed position for their conversation.

He wasn't holding court in his usual manner. A hometown hero, Ches Murphy never missed an opportunity to press rewind on a game-winning touchdown from his college days. Rather than lead the conversation, he appeared to be the recipient of a message. His hands remained tight in his pockets while he answered with a few agreeable nods between occasional glances in our group's direction. Their conversation ended with a firm handshake. And Ches looked at us once again before opening the gate.

I was certain we'd violated a crowd ordinance during COVID procedures. Our gathering was sizably over the ten-person limit, and Ches's wife, Twila, refused to wear a mask. Grey and Higgs greeted the officers for their oldest brother who was in his fixed position at the grill. While the policemen's patent leather shoes crunched the pebbled walk, Uncle Weyman flipped meat over the coals. He looked up once, flicking his spatula at Vy who was standing in the doorway, holding a plate of hamburger buns. On cue, she shuttled inside and pulled the curtain closed.

My stepdad turned his palms toward the sky, standing in front of the two officers, trading glances at his brother who shifted his weight on his feet. This wasn't Grey's typical easy-going manner; I felt confident he was defending his frail mother's reputation for being a rule-breaker. He returned his hands to his hips and widened his stance. His brother gently tapped Grey's chest and whispered something. Then, my stepdad tucked his hands in his pockets, lowered his head, and turned to face the kids making waves in the pool.

The officers lapped the pool deck scanning each person on their way past the diving board and jacuzzi. I blinked my eyes a few times. In the shade of a magnolia tree, Twila peered over the top of her book, shielding her unmasked face, as the policeman approached her chaise. With a tip of their hats in her direction, the duo appeared to be doing more than enforcing COVID policies. My trembling fingers traced the edges of my mother's peach-colored nails and followed the soft rounded edge of her elbow. I stared at her chiseled shoulders and jawline up to her caramel circles hovering over her rounded cheeks. This was the way I wanted to remember her: healthy, smiling, and worry-free. For fear the next time I'd see her, she'd be decrepit and gray. My fourteen-year-old heart tore between wanting to save her and kill her in the same breath.

"My namesake," RaRa said, prompting my gaze into her furrowed brow. "This is for you and Olivia."

The claps of standard-issued shoes grew nearer, and I felt RaRa's hand rest on mine. I prepared myself to watch my mother shackled and read her Miranda rights, as I'd seen on true crime documentaries. Then, I'd listen to the plan of how my sister and I would be raised by my grandmother in hopes of not becoming wayward orphans.

She turned on her heel and stepped toward the policemen, her silver bob shifting as she raised her chin with their approach. Their group mumbled; my ears strained to hear. I watched as something spurred a gentle laugh in their huddle, then RaRa slid her candy-colored accessories up her straightened arms. Her pale, bony wrists stretched in front of her. Olivia stood in the shallow end with the other kids, resting her hands on toys bobbing beside her.

The grease from the grill stopped flaring. Music dimmed, and my mother's inhale was all that filled my ears.

"Rosalyn Irvine." The officer's tone flattened. "You're under arrest—"

His words morphed into garbled syllables. I flung my hands over my paper mask pushing it closer to my gaping mouth.

Air passed through the soaked covering, over my fingers and I lifted my eyes to see my mother standing beside me with her arms folded across her chest. Her face was flat, her eyes fixed, and her chin firm. She studied the scene emotionless.

Stepping toward RaRa, I said, "What's happening?"

"I've mishandled some affairs, it seems," RaRa said, leaning toward me. My fingers outlined the edges of the handcuffs as tears filled my eyes. "None of that, dear. I'll be fine."

"But are you going to jail?" I whimpered.

With a shrug, she said, "Possibly."

"Why? What's going on?"

"I'll be fine dear. We'll get this cleared up, and we'll see each other again soon. Don't forget how to make those Tom Collins I like. I'll need one when I get out."

Holding RaRa's hand, I looked at Mom over my shoulder. She stared at her shackled mother as if she was selecting a meat and three from a cafeteria menu. It was identical to her emotionless gaze from the front porch that fueled my rage just hours before. I returned to RaRa. "But jail is dirty. It's not safe. Will you be okay?"

"Of course, dear," she said, tossing her jagged bangs to the side. "They can't eat me for supper."

***

Mom spared Olivia and me from the details of RaRa's arrest. We were told she'd done some "funny math" with her taxes. She was sent to the women's penitentiary in Boston. RaRa never came back for the Tom Collins drink she coveted. I begged Mom to let me see her, but she refused without justification.

I made the mistake of sharing my theory with my therapist. She convinced me I was on a witch hunt against my mother. I didn't truly believe she'd murdered my father, rather, I was seeking somewhere to direct my teenage angst. She said it was common for teens to push away from the same-sex parent. Eventually, I accepted what was presented: my father's death was a suicide, and my grandmother was imprisoned for tax evasion.

At some point, I admit, I was relieved believing it wasn't Mom. I didn't have to move, change schools, or find new friends again. If Mom had been arrested, could Grey or RaRa have managed Liv's blood sugars? Would Aunt Tish have taken us in? My life was already a soap opera in my hometown, the last thing I needed was my mother behind bars.

Olivia and I fell into our high school routines: band practice, proms, and hanging out with friends. My family drama won me a few "Wows" and "What the fucks" with the other teenagers. Somehow, we found a way to use it as an awkward conversation starter.

It didn't take much to convince Taylor to get out of town after graduation. Berklee College of Music was an obvious choice given our passion for the arts, but for me, it was about being in Boston.

I knew once I turned eighteen, Mom couldn't stop me from seeing RaRa. My heart ached to hear her side of the story. I agonized to hear the truth.

"Your family drama kept me out of prison, I can always thank you for that," I say.

"And what can I thank you for?" Taylor asks.

"For finding your dad." My voice raises, and I'm unsure why she's still ungrateful for my investigation after all these years.

"I knew who my dad was the whole time. I didn't need you to share it with the world."

"Look, I just knew that we were more than friends. Tish and my family grew up together, which was cool, but there was always a closeness that I couldn't explain."

"Not everything needs splanin.'"

"Can I call you Aunt Tay?"

"If you want me to knock your teeth out, go for it."

"Don't you ever want to run into his arms and tell him how much you love him?"

"Hell, yeah, I do, but Moms and I like to keep our life private. We're not like the Cameks!"

"Yeah, we like ours on a billboard."

"Look, my mother is an upstanding businesswoman. She doesn't want people to know she was the mistress to the most prominent figure in town."

"But they love each other and have loved each other for decades."

"Moms is tough, but she has her limits."

"It's town talk. They move on to someone or something else eventually."

"The Piedmonts have been the talk of the town for a long time, I mean until the Camek girls came around." My friend huffs a laugh. "Nineteen years ago, Moms lost clients when she had a bastard child." Taylor's eyes widen in my direction. "Then, she lost more when it was obvious I was a mixed chick." They point to their bouncing coils. "Now, she has to explain my pronoun preference to them, and you're suggesting she share the name of her lover that was a married white man twenty-five years older?" Taylor shutters. "That's bankruptcy for Tish."

"Ms. Twila's been dead for years now."

"If my dad was a chump, maybe it would go unnoticed. But we're talking about Ches Murphy, Alabama football star and self-made millionaire." Taylor's curls shake toward the floor. "Can you say, run out of town? And that's if we're lucky."

"But he loves her, you. Both of you, so much. It's easy to see he regrets missing out on your life."

Taylor walks to the window, moves the flower vases to the side, and rests their butt on the ledge. "She surprised me tonight. I didn't realize she dated Uncle Weyman," I say.

My roommate arches their eyebrows in my direction. "It didn't work out. Her dad came down hard on her for dating a white dude, so even if there was chemistry there, it never would have happened. She resolved to stay friends with the Murphy boys."

"But Ches?"

"After their graduation, Weyman and Higgs joined the military, Grey moved to his grandparents' farm. Moms didn't have a reason to hang out at the Murphy house." Taylor fidgets with the buttons on their flannel shirt. "Years later, he randomly showed up at her salon one day."

"And they were both adults." My shoulders sway side to side.

"Right, but he was still married," says Taylor, wagging their finger at me. "It was fine, she knew her father would never approve."

"But then Mr. Piedmont passed."

"May he rest in peace." Taylor looks down to the floor tiles. "Moms kept cutting Ches's hair and they kept talking." Their eyes widen with their smile as they slap their thighs. "And God gifted the world with yours truly."

"I think everyone in the family knows you're my aunt."

"I will punch you." Taylor gives me their famous side-eye. "Besides, it's not up to me."

"Your dad's spent every Christmas and birthday across the street at Uncle Weyman's house, watching you open your gifts through the living room window."

"Mothers are complicated."

That's an understatement.

We suspect he bought Tish's house for her and Taylor too. It's no coincidence after Taylor was born, the county's premier hairstylist opened a new salon and moved into the house directly across from Ches's son and daughter-in-law. Also, sus, Ches lives in a mansion on the edge of town, but every Murphy family event takes place at his son's three-bedroom ranch-style home. Vy thinks it's because we love her cooking; we all have our secrets.

As a kid, Ches attended every one of our band concerts and charity fundraisers. In high school, he chaperoned dances, hosted graduation parties, and offered unsolicited advice to the head football coach on the regular. Olivia and I didn't know any different. To us, he joined the ranks of 'super-grands' with RaRa and Mama Rose. It was later when I recognized Ches as a committed father who knew protecting his child meant watching them grow up from the sidelines.

CHAPTER FOURTEEN

Lennon

The weekend Taylor and I moved into 150 Mass, Ches went with us. We had a ton to unpack. I didn't care whose dad tagged along to college if they were willing to lug boxes eight floors. He made one trip, then tipped some fraternity pledge to do the rest. After move-in was over, Mom stayed in Boston for an extra day while Ches and Tish rode back together.

The regional women's correctional center was ninety miles from the college. Hell, I mapped it before I knew my class schedule. I begged her to let me see RaRa.

"I'm sure I'll regret it," she said, sifting through her purse. "But I know you'll go on your own anyways."

My glasses fogged stepping out of dorm lobby. Wiping the lenses on my shirt, I was surprised Massachusetts humidity rivaled the 'air you can wear' from home. Once inside Mom's van, I blasted Olivia Rodrigo in my headphones and waited for her to tell me it's too loud. She didn't. The dash clock read 7:30. 9:00 was visitor check-in. Mom fastened her seat belt. Her face was stark. My mouth opened to advise her of the time, but I opted not to push my luck with more demands. Besides, Mom's never late.

Three flags waved across the sapphire sky stretched from stacked buildings surrounded by barbed wire fencing. It resembled my high school. I chuckled, relieved I wasn't returning. Mom tapped my thigh parking the car and my stomach pitted.

The hum of cars on the freeway muffled behind me. A blanket of silence fell between Mom and I walking across the parking lot.

Our approach signaled the glass doors to open and sterile air flooded my mouth and nose.

A uniformed woman wearing a black Kevlar vest spoke to us. "Sign the visitor registration form, please."

"Is it okay for my daughter to go in without me?" Mom asked.

"Is she eighteen or older?"

"Yes."

"Lady, she can do whatever she wants without you," she said, stretching the vowels longer than the southern drawls I was accustomed to. Her top knot and wide eyes peered over Mom's shoulder, to me, as she her fingers in tapped her palm. "Baby, come here and sign your name."

I stared at the tiles beneath my boots.

"Len?" Mom faced me. "Do you still want to do this? Maybe you and I can just talk—"

Lugging my foot forward, I maneuvered around her to greet the officer at the desk.

"Sign your full name here," the clerk said, handing me a pen. "I'll need to see your ID, also."

I fumbled with my license while Mom took a seat near the Coke machine. "I'll wait here."

"You're a long way from home," the clerk said, handing me my ID.

"Yes, I-I'm uh..." I stammered. "I'm a student...at Berklee."

"Okay, well get a Sox hat as soon as possible, and we'll forgive the southern accent," she said, flashing a wink in my direction.

"We call them beanies at home, but 'sock hat' will grow on me, I guess."

The officer scrunched her thick, black eyebrows together.

"I love winter. I can't wait to shop for new clothes." My voice volleyed up and down, as I attempted to normalize my surroundings.

Her lips pressed together. "If you have any personal belongings, leave them in a locker or with your mother."

My vape pen pressed against my palm as I patted my pockets. The guard stared at the bead of sweat dripping from my temple.

I smiled, and walked toward Mom. "Can you hold this for me?" Rolling her eyes, she removed the metal tube from my hand and placed it in her purse.

"Did you tell Taylor where you were going today?" she asked.

Searching my other pockets, I said, "I mentioned it."

"Did she have questions?"

"Not really. I mean, Tay knows it's something I've wanted to do for a long time."

The guard tapped on the desk.

"Len," Mom said, gently tugging my wrist. "There's nothing a mother wouldn't do for her child. Just know that."

I creased my forehead, and her hand relaxed into her lap.

After passing through the metal detector, the officer's wand waved over my belt buckle. An obnoxious alert signaled mom's returning to the desk to retrieve another item I wasn't able to identify as contraband.

Maybe I'm not ready to go in, I thought.

The guard continued her safety check, and I was reminded of all the times we waited for Olivia to complete a thorough check by airport security with each trip to see Mom or Dad. The TSA officers never knew what to do about my sister's insulin pump. She got the full terrorist pat-down for a life-saving device with every trip.

A visitor's badge looped around my neck, and I followed the hallway to the inmate visiting area. A lock clanked behind me. The door slid open in sync with my arrival. Round wooden tables were perfectly spaced around the room; orange chairs sat on opposite ends with a freestanding plexiglass barrier in the center. A plump, uniformed man directed me to a table in the far corner of the room.

"Keep your hands where I can see them at all times, understood?" he bellowed.

My head bounced on my shoulders, and I clasped my fingers together in plain view. One table over, a woman bounced an infant in her lap. The baby's cooing filled the otherwise gloomy room. At the next table, a man sat with his hands like mine, folded on the surface. The halogen light reflected off his bald head. His lip twitched watching other families trickle in the doorway. My lip tucked between my teeth matching his and, for a minute, I wished Mom was with me. The door clanked shut, and the walls of the tomb enclosed.

From behind the desk, the officer called to us. "Visitors, the inmates will now enter the room. There is one hug allowed when they arrive at your table, and there is one hug allowed when it's time for them to exit. When speaking to the inmate, do not use profanity or derogatory language. Do not hold hands. Do not reach around the plexiglass barrier. Do not attempt to give the inmate any items. Any of these acts will have you immediately removed from the visitor's room and the inmate will return to their cell. Are there any questions?"

I had questions: Why was my heart is racing? Why were my palms sticking together? Why was I the one who felt like a caged animal? My teeth peeled skin from around my cuticle, and the officer darted his eyes in my direction. With laced fingers on top of the table again, I bit my bottom lip and, like everyone else, watched the other door.

"Inmates, enter."

A round woman entered wearing a forest green top with matching pants. She waddled around tables before stopping at the bald guy. His hands unlatched and the couple gripped each other. His shirt wrinkled in her grasp prompting the guard to clear his throat until the couple released their embrace

My attention returned to the room's entrance. Another woman, in matching top and bottoms, filled the doorway. Her layered blonde bangs contrasted against her leathery forehead and paper-thin skin. She flashed a sideways smile in my direction. The floor creaked with each footstep. Thick folds of skin jiggled under her sleeve as she stretched her arms wide. My burning eyes focused on her pudgy round feet, crammed into white tennis shoes like two navy beans. A young voice squealed, and the giant footsteps stopped. I raised my head to see her clutching a toddler, swinging him side to side.

Another inmate stepped into the room. Her gray highlights blended into faded red corkscrew curls piled atop her head. Her emerald eyes fixed in my direction. Four years had passed since I saw RaRa. My head tilted as the woman wove her way around the chairs, to the young mother and the cooing baby. I straightened my hunched spine and moved to the end of the chair.

Women of random ages, some not much older than me, entered the room one by one. I stretched my neck to see the door closing behind a woman at the end of the queue. Her long silver strands rested on her shoulders. The creases around her lips deepened with her smug look to the guard. She nodded passing each seated inmate and their visitors along her path.

At my table, her raspy voice deadened. "Don't get up, my dear," she said. "They don't like the peasants getting a lot of attention."

"Ra Ra—"

One hand covered her chest as she used the other to adjust her chair. "My heart is too old for such sentiment." She pulled her top lip inward. "Besides, revered nicknames are meant for the deserving." The green eyes that once dazzled were barely visible around her oversized, black rimmed glasses.

"You're an adult now, I see."

"Yes, mam."

"Roz will be fine."

"R-Roz?" I stutter, feeling the word come from my lips. "Thanks for seeing me today."

"Well, you lucked out." Her yellow tinged fingernails tapped the tabletop. "The King of Siam canceled. Something about how the high mold count aggravates his allergies, you know Royalty." Her hand flared, sending a wave of nostalgia to hear her jeweled arms jingle.

My cheeks tightened, and I forced my lips together. I wanted to smell her Moroccan rose perfume again. I was desperate to see her cherry-red lipstick leave marks on her cigarette and the sweating glass of a Tom Collins. Rather, my fashionista grandmother had traded her luxurious wardrobe for a jumpsuit that sagged on her shoulders like an old quilt.

"Our time is limited, Lennon Rosalyn, and I'm deathly curious what brings you to Westchester. Surely, the chowder in Boston satiates your curious pallet." Her "ERs" stretched into "AHs."

"I...I'm not sure where to begin." My face warmed.

"Is your mother with you?"

"Yes."

"Krissy wouldn't dare let her firstborn come into these walls unattended. Well done, you," she said, with a tilt of her head toward the exit. She touched her lips like she's missing a smoke, then clicked her fingertips together. "Yet she saw no need to enter the doors herself." She stared at me.

"Did you come to see for yourself they, indeed, have not eaten me for supper?" she asked, flashing a smirk in my direction.

Raising my eyes to meet hers, I said, "I...I want to know why you're really here?"

"What does it matter? A jury of my peers tried and sentenced me years ago. Now, I'm living the remainder of my days on Earth in this tuna can," she resigned. "You've obviously moved on with your life. Have you entered college, yet?"

"Berklee," I said, looking down at the woodgrain table.

"And not the great University of Alabama?" Her hands waved over her head and the guard noticed her demonstration "I'm sure your mother's distraught you opted for an out of a state college curriculum."

"She knows I love music."

"There are closer music schools, my dear."

"Well, you grew up here and I, I guess I've listened to your stories for so long...Boston intrigues me."

"A wonder indeed," she said, tilting her head. "So, you've moved on in life, but still have questions about my arrest. Didn't your mother tell you?"

"She said it was something with your taxes."

"Why do you *think* I'm here?"

"I...I think you may know something about my dad's death." A tiny drop of spit dangled on my lip, forcing me to wipe it with my knuckle.

"Like what, pray tell?"

"I...I think you, or Mom, or both of you, had something to do with it. I want you to tell me the truth."

"Those are bold accusations." Her fingernails tapped together. "What will knowing do?"

"Give me peace."

"From what? You've done nothing to warrant discord."

"I have nightmares...about Dad dying...in the hotel room...alone."

"Sounds like a luxurious way to go, compared to...here." She looked beyond the rim of her glasses around the room. "Surrounded by friends, of course."

"I think Dad's dead because of me."

Roz nods. "Say more."

"I think you killed Dad to avenge your grandchildren. Is that it? Tell me, did I drive you to do this?" I tampered my voice before the guard acknowledged me.

"You make me too much of a martyr, my dear," she said, leaning back in her chair. "I signed the contract because your father was a tyrant, a bully, a coward—"

"Okay, so you didn't like Dad and you wanted me and Liv to live with Mom." Her head tilted at my assumption. "You didn't think there was any other way to beat the legal system? So you found a way to remove him from the picture on your own."

"I've never been one to play by the rules."

"But—" I looked at the others around us and leaned close to the glass barrier between us. "At the cookout, you handed Mom a phone. You said something that made me think the job you ordered, didn't go down as planned."

A thin-lipped smile inches across her face. "Your memory is impeccable."

Surprised to be accused of being a good historian, I continued. "If it didn't happen the way you ordered it, then how?"

"I thought you wanted to know the *why*. You have it. I ordered a murder on your father because I didn't think your mom had the balls to do it herself." She scowled at the breastfeeding baby behind her. The mother pulled a blanket around them both. "But Krissy always loved to prove me wrong."

My chest thuds.

"Like mother, like daughter, I guess." She smirked. "Quite simply, Krissy's plan played out before mine."

My eyes widened seeing the droplets leave my mouth and land on the window between us. "On the porch, at Mom's house before the Fourth of July party—"

"I gave your mother a way out."

"But you said your plan didn't go through."

"It didn't," she said. "My ex-son-in-law was dead and that's all that really mattered."

I forced a swallow.

"Krissy was crippled by love and forgiveness, so even at the depths of her depression after losing you, I didn't think she'd take drastic action to get you back." Roz took in a deep breath. "When I knew my contract was still open, I suspected Krissy conjured up our Kelly spirit. Then, at the funeral, his wife Patton—"

"Peyton."

"Whatever. Your mom's reaction to her accusations reassured me—"

"She already knew."

"My namesake," RaRa purred, tilting her head in my direction. "It sounds like you thought the same."

"So, why let the police arrest you."

"Because there's nothing a mother won't do for her daughter."

The room attendant announced we had fifteen minutes left. RaRa rolled her eyes in response.

"Then you're saying you just took one for the team? I'm not buying it."

"You and your sister returned to your father's house after Christmas. Krissy was inconsolable. We took turns staying with her. A suicide watch, if you will." I bit my lip. "Olivia's incident had come to light, and the family struggled to formulate a united plan of action."

"That's when I told Aunt Audrie everything, I guess she went back to Mom."

"Au contraire. Audrie didn't think Krissy could the job either. Your aunt and I formed an alliance. We wanted your mother to raise you free of his ridicule and trifling put-downs. Audrie and I designed a plan to get rid of him for good and protect your mother's innocence."

"Why protect her?"

"How could she care for you and your sister from these walls? Having her incarcerated defeated the purpose. We needed her to return to the impeccable parent she'd always been."

"Why would you sacrifice your freedom for Mom?"

"This may come as a surprise to you, but...I wasn't the best mother." She leaned back in her seat, prompting the young mother behind her to scooch her chair forward. "I did a lot of things to keep your mom from having a relationship with her own father.

A lot of unflattering things, all to protect my ego, my self-worth, my...position in her life."

"Like what?"

"Brutally sacrificing a toy her new stepmother gave her, comes to mind. There were photos, birthday cards, and other trinkets I tossed into the fire when Krissy wasn't looking. I encouraged her to lie to her father, spy on her stepmother, and ultimately prove her loyalty to me by rejecting him."

"Holy shit!" Her discerning look stopped me. "Sorry."

"Shocking, I know," she said, relaxing her brow. "I'm not sure I ever healed from divorcing Krissy's father, but when I saw the way my son-in-law alienated you from your mother, I recognized his tactics as my own. Keeping my child from her father was the only thing I ever regretted." She adjusted herself in her chair and leaned closer to me. Water pooled in the corner of her eyes. "I watched her go through failed marriages, eating disorders, and depression. She recovered from many tragedies in her life, but your absence rocked her to the core. Your mother's life hung in the balance, and I knew her only reason for living was you and your sister." Inhaling air through her nose with a huff, she looked to the fluttering light above us.

"Five minutes," the officer called from over my shoulder.

"But you'll never leave here."

"I'm a battle-ax, kid." She adjusted her glasses on her nose. "You don't need to worry about me. Besides, Melanie and I..." she said, tilting her head toward the red-and-white striped bun behind her. "We run the library together." Lifting her chin, she shrugged her shoulders. "It's not Tuscany, but it's an easy retirement."

"Why didn't Mom tell me the truth about your arrest?"

"I'm sure she wanted to spare you more grief. Tell me, is your life any easier now that you know your mother is a murderer? Why not just believe it was me and justice has been served? It's a fairytale ending if you think about it."

"I...I forgive you. For what it's worth, I do. I don't know how I'd react in that situation, but I'm sure you did the best you could."

Surrounding chatter filled the room as the other visitors took full advantage of the second, and final, opportunity to hug their loved ones. "You're just like your mother, such a sweet girl. Stay that way, kiddo. Don't let the world harden you as it has me. Bitterness leads to loneliness, every time."

I nod.

"Do me a favor, would ya?" she asked. "Let me know when my credit gets cashed."

"It's still out there? How will I—"

"Watch the Olympics," she said, pushing her chair under the table's edge. "You'll know."

***

My muscles ache repositioning myself in the chair. Popping joints along my spine realign as I shift each hip. I slide my hand across my face, making my eyelids smack together. The haze clears and the overhead lights reflect off a smooth face at my sister's bedside. I jump to the edge of the chair.

"Good morning," she says. I drag my hand across my face again. "I'm collecting your sister's blood work for the laboratory. Did you get any sleep?" She glances in my direction and smirks. "Don't answer that. I have some assessment skills even though I'm not technically a nurse yet."

The young woman lifts her basket of vampire tools from the bedside table and a growl rumbles from the opposite corner. "Well, someone got comfortable."

My eyes roll hearing my roommate shift into a different gear. "Taylor could sleep through an apocalypse." The girl gives a one-beat laugh. "Hey, do you think the docs will take my sister off this breathing machine today?" I ask, nodding my head toward the human resembling backside of a stereo.

"I haven't received report yet, but I'll ask my instructor. She's at the front desk now."

"Oh, you're a student. I should have recognized the badge."

"Yeah. Are you in nursing school, too?" she asks.

"God no. I can't keep plants alive, much less humans." I snort. "I mean...no, our mom, this is my sister, we share a mom—"

The student's thick brows raise.

"I'm sorry, it's early."

"It's okay, I understand."

"Our mom is like the best nurse ever. She's won all sorts of awards and recognition. She's got a lot of clout. I knew I'd never be the nurse she is, so I didn't even try. Any medical knowledge I have is from my sister's medical condition."

"Cool. So, what's your thing?"

"Music. I'm at Berklee." Noticing her blank stare. "The one in Boston, not California," I say, wondering how anyone can stand to be in the room with me.

"That's awesome. I failed music when we had to play the recorder."

We both laugh as she leans toward the glass window behind me. Following her gaze, I squint to make out the dim shadows surrounding the front desk. It's shift change. Fresh, well-rested staff enter wearing sweaters. Their cheeks still pink from the crisp fall morning. The nightshift team roll their shoulders and stretch, waking up for final rounds. She points her pen toward the desk. "She's here, I'll ask about your sister's treatment plan first. Ms. Murphy is so smart, she'll know what is going on."

"Ms. Mur—"

"Murphey. Do you know her?"

"Uh, no. Not at all. Thanks again for letting me know the plan." I stand from my seat, placing my hands on my hips. My fingertips pat the vial secured by my waistband.

"I got lucky with her as my clinical instructor. She's different from the other professors. She's smart, but she doesn't make you feel like a dumbass. Can I say that?"

"Sure." My neck stiffens. "We speak fluent sarcasm in here."

"Yeah, we do," Taylor mumbles, reaching their arms over their head, followed by a deep yawn. "What time is it?"

"6 A.M.," the student says. "Let me get these to the lab, and we'll know how close we are to getting Miss Olivia out of here."

The nursing student places three tubes filled with my sister's blood in her pocket and slides the glass door closed behind her. Her starched white pants are all that's visible to me as they fade into the dimly lit workstation.

"Sorry, I must have dozed off."

"Wish I could have," I say, staring at the desk. "I keep thinking about seeing RaRa in jail."

"Yikes," Taylor says. "Wasn't once enough?"

I shake my head and return to twisting the kinks in my back. "I'm sure it's on my mind today since we're in Mom's backyard."

Taylor nods.

"I wanted to go back to see Roz—cause unanswered questions, ya know—but I didn't want to push my luck either. We said what we needed to say, I guess. Besides, it wasn't long after our talk that...." I clear my throat. "Well, you know...Roz did the ultimate bailout."

"Wow," Taylor says. "Just left this world and never got her money back for a botched murder for hire."

"Oh, she had a credit," I say, hearing my back pop into position. My muscles relax as I hunch forward feeling a pinch then a sting. "Ouch! Shit!"

"What happened?"

A warm thick fluid returns. I press my shirt into my stomach where I think the cut is. "Nothing. My back, I fell asleep in a weird position."

Taylor stands from the sofa. "Here, let me help you."

My body jerks upright. "I'm fine, really," I say. "Yeah. Roz had a death credit; didn't I tell you?"

Their lips close, and they ease toward me at the edge of Liv's bed. "Like, an eye-for-an-eye credit? An I-need-to-find-another-roommate credit?"

I flip my wrist in her direction. "You're fine."

"You just told me Rosalyn Irvine, O.G. Rosalyn Kelly, of the Boston Mafia Kelly's, has an uncashed check for someone's behind."

"I didn't say it was uncashed." My best friend tilts her head to me. "Remember when watched the Olympics?"

"Kind of. I don't know, Len. You make me watch a lot of shit I don't like. I usually just zone out," Taylor says, using their fingers to pick their curls.

"They were in Paris," I say. Taylor's face is blanker than usual. "I made you watch it because we want to live in Paris after college, remember?"

"Okay, yeah. It's coming back to me." Their head bobs up and down.

"A news anchor reported the daughter of a wealthy horse trainer died in a freak accident." My lips pinch together, and I tilt my chin down. "She was warming up the horse for a dressage competition when the horse reared up, dumping onto her neck." I give two forced blinks in her direction.

"I'd be lying if I told you I stayed awake during all those events you made me watch. I mean, dancing horses in little hats, I just—"

"The woman was Peyton."

My friend's mouth gapes open again. "Peyton Camek?"

"Minchew. She took her maiden name back after Dad died. It was more recognizable to the public."

"Okay, so...accidents happen. Especially with a two-thousand-pound beast who's frazzled from traveling the Atlantic."

"P was an experienced horsewoman," I say, shaking my head. "She never would have ever gone out that way. An accident of that magnitude would have been too damaging to the family name. Legendary horse breeders can't say their daughter made a rookie mistake handling a prize-winning champion."

"So, you think Roz—"

I nod my head, slowly removing my fingers from the cut while holding the vial in place under my skirt. "She had the final word."

The lights flicker on at the nursing station, and my eyes dart back to the window. Activity increases behind the desk. More scrub tops come into view, as staff shed their cardigans from their shoulders. Monitors glow in their reading glasses, and pens emerge from their topknots as they make notes for their shift. One nurse's crimson bun loosens with her retrieval of a black pen nested at the base.

She walks to the glass box on the wall and reaches inside retrieving a clear canister. Much like the ones at the bank that Olivia and I would fight to open for the coveted lollipop inside. The nurse empties the canister while nodding in response to someone speaking in her direction. She turns toward the room. Her pink lip balm glistens in the warming fluorescent lights, and our eyes meet.

The thud against my chest wall grows louder. She returns to giving thoughtful nods to her peer in between scribbling notes as the tube shoots back up through the vacuum system. It's the barbeque all over again, only this time, there's no Roz to take the fall. My neck loosens as I turn to Olivia in the bed.

"Looks like the day shift is coming in," says Taylor.

My hand runs across the inside pocket of my skirt, fumbling over the stickiness to retrieve the medicine vial.

"The *real* nurse will be in soon to give a full update, I bet," my friend says, standing in front of the window with their hands on both hips.

Perfect.

CHAPTER FIFTEEN

Olivia

The bed dips, and I'm burdened again with perpetual burning in the back of my throat. My eyes peel open and I strain to see blurred images across the room. My sister's roommate is standing with both hands on their hips, a blanket draped around their back and shoulders. Someone is rummaging in the corner beside me. My neck stiffens with my attempt to look in that direction. Pressure fills my voice box, but the air movement is stunted by the bulb sitting at the base of my throat. Chimes flood my ear beside me. A swoosh of forced air hits my lungs.

"What are you looking for in Liv's things?" Taylor asks, looking into the corner of the room closest to my bed.

That had better not be my Louis Vuitton.

"Lennon." Taylor's voice thickens. "What are you doing?"

My sister steps into my periphery. Light streams through an opening in the curtain, she uses it to illuminate a clear vial. Using her teeth, she pinches the orange cap from one of my insulin syringes and places the needle against the bottom of the bottle.

"Nothing you need to worry about," she says, the cap dangling from her lip. With two firm flicks against the syringe, air bubbles to the top and she expresses liquid from the needle.

"Have things gotten this bad, Len?" Taylor asks. "I know you've struggled at school this semester, and your sis and all, but are you ready for this level of high?"

Capping the needle, she folds the syringe inside her palm and tucks it into the pocket of her T-shirt. "It's not for me," she says, strolling across the room. I hear a glass clink, and the plastic thud of the levered door for the sharps container.

"Well, *I'm* not ready for that mess." Taylor shakes their head, removing a buzzing phone from their back pocket. "Who's hitting me up this early?" They mumble. "It's Moms. She's outside the unit with doughnuts for the staff."

Get back in the game, Tay! Lennon has a loaded needle filled with a mystery med she is not qualified to administer.

My sister ignores our friend's announcement and continues staring at the nurses' station. The flickering light brightens her face. Shadows circulate outside the glass door.

"Did you hear me?" Taylor asks.

"Yeah, doughnuts. Sounds good."

"I'm gonna help her with the door, you good? You're acting a little squirrelly, my girl, not gonna lie."

Lennon nods, pulling the curtain open for Taylor to exit.

"Okay, well you stand there and look weird. I'll go do everything else," Taylor says. Before exiting, they glance in my direction. "Hey, look whose eyes are open."

My eyes widen despite feeling like their staring into a broiling oven. Lennon's head jerks. "Liv. It's me, Lennon," she says. I flutter my eyelids fighting to keep them open. "I think she sees me."

"Of course, she does. She seems me to," Taylor says.

They gawk at me as if I'm a lost puppy, inching closer to my face than I'm comfortable with. I nod my head.

"Just stay relaxed, okay?" Leaning over the bedrail, the rounded edge of the while plunger in her shirt pocket comes into view. "If you stay calm, I bet they take this tube out. None of that coughing and thrashing around, okay? I know you like to be dramatic and all—"

Me? You're the one walking around with a lethal injection in your pocket.

"Olivia?"

"Imma be right back with some do-nuts." Taylor's mouth rounds with every syllable and I wonder do they think I've lost my understanding of the English language. "You got to get that tube out to have one. I bet Mama Tish got your favorite, Boston Cream." The door slides close silencing the room.

Len's gentle touch pats my head, forcing my eyes to close. "It's all going to be okay. Nobody can hurt you anymore. I'm here."

Flinging them open again, I notice the pencil-thin edges of her eyelids are blistered. Blood vessels creep in from the sides of her swollen stare, and broken capillaries flood her flat cheeks. She hovers closer.

"Mom did this to you." Pausing, her skeleton gaze shutters toward the speaker on my bedrail. "Just like she did to Dad. She's poisoning you." Her head nods in response to her statement. "Your insulin. Does she still pick it up from the hospital apothecary?" Lennon affirms for me. "Mom probably says it's so she can apply her hospital discount." Rubbing my shoulders, she says, "She's having it remixed. Stronger, I bet." Her fingers trace the IV in my hand. "So, when you give yourself a dose, it's ten times more." My heart pounds. "She's messing with my sister, and I'm about to make up for what I've done."

The tweets from the overhead monitor keep time with my heart. Faster and faster, it races inside my chest as my helplessness blankets me.

"Listen, I know it was my fault Dad died."

No, you're very wrong.

Her voice muffles in the sheets, "But I won't lose you too."

My hand finds the strength to touch her tangled hair, and her body shakes with every sob. Tears soak into cold wet spot on my chest. I've got to tell her she's wrong. She's irrationally filled with guilt that should have never been hers to own.

Please don't do whatever it is you're about to do.

Lifting her head, she turns to me. Her cracked lips part as she says, "Mom's outside at the desk and I think she's going to come in and check on you." My fingers grasp for her hair, but she pulls the strands out of my reach. "What I'm about to do is to help you. Killing her may send me to jail, but you'll be able to live your life. Free from fear that she'll hurt you again—"

My hands tighten. The muscles in my arm feel like they're tearing apart as I lift my hands closer to my face. My elbow straightens, shoving Lennon off of me while my other hand grasps the breathing tube.

"Stop!" Lennon shouts.

Like lifting a pallet of bricks, I lean forward. My head pounds. I tug. The tube stops; it's stuck.

"Olivia, quit it! You're hurting yourself!"

I tug harder. A ring of fire surrounds the lump in my throat. The burning is more than I can breathe through. Alarms blare. Again, I snatch the tube forward, this time ripping tape from the corner of my lips.

Lennon leaves my bed and runs to the door. "Help! We need help in here."

What feels like a hardboiled egg regurgitates through my mouth and over my tongue just as I feel cool air rush in and I gasp for air, "Len—" Lava runs over my vocal cords. I hold my hand out to touch her arm and widen my eyes.

"She's got it out," a woman's voice says. My focus adjusts to examine the blood-tinged tube lying on my chest. "Call respiratory and get a non-rebreather mask for her, stat."

"On it," a voice from the squawk box answers.

"Mom—" my voice scratches.

Reaching over my head, she says, "Don't talk. Let your lungs breathe a minute." A plastic mask covers my nose and mouth and oxygen rushes in.

"Mom," I say, feeling my words vibrate the mask.

"Shhh," she says. "We have a lot to talk about later."

The alarms silence with every pull and pop behind me. She brushes my hair out of my eyes with a wet washcloth. A wave of her lavender body wash, the one I gave her for her birthday, saturates my senses only to be replaced by cold air circulating. I crinkle my nose. Her lips press against my forehead.

The bed raises to support my head, and I sink into the pillow behind me. "That feels better, doesn't it?" she asks.

I nod. Weakness blankets my face.

"You're getting stronger every day, Livvy."

"I think the doctor will agree it was time to come off this thing. We could have done it in a less traumatic way, but you know our family likes to rip the band-aid, don't we?"

Family. My eyes fling open.

"You've had a lot of visitors," she says, pulling away from me. She walks toward the end of my bed. "Thank you for making the trip, Lennon." Her hip leans into the footboard. "How've you been?"

My sister stands frozen against the wall. She offers no response.

"That was a lot to watch your sister go through. You look frightened. Want to talk about it?"

Her feet pound on the sticky floor, and Mom's body bends onto the mattress beside my legs. The locked wheels glide us sideways for a second.

Mom's hand thrashes forward. "What are you doing?" Mom forces her words out. Lennon's body smacks against hers pushing Mom further into the mattress.

The washcloth Mom used to cool me jostles loose from my forehead. It rolls down my shoulder, plopping onto my wrist.

Heaving Len forward by her shoulders, Mom shouts, "Stop this!" Her body falls to the floor. Len straddles her pausing to remove the syringe cap with her teeth.

I bend my fingers in all directions until I snag a corner of the cloth and reel it into my fist. With a fling of my wrist, the white blob wobbles through the air hitting Len's shoulder. It's enough to make my sister look in my direction. Mom grabs Lennon's clenched fist, barely missing the exposed needle. My fingers scramble to find the call button on the guardrail.

"What's going on?" Vy asks.

Mom shoves Lennon to the ground.

"Do I need to send security?" Vy asks.

The stones in my throat rattle a garbled plea, "Yes!"

Beep, boop.

My mom and sister glare at each other, both pacing their breath. Mom's elbows rest on her thighs. "I know you've been under a lot of stress."

"Stress *you* caused!"

"Settle down so we can talk about this." Mom pushes her hands on her thighs to stand. Reaching her hand to Lennon on the floor, she says, "I love you. I've always loved you and I always will."

"Don't try this shit, Mom. I know what you did to Dad, and I know what you're doing to my sister."

"I'm sure you're hurting. We have a lot to talk about. Let's not make things worse by fighting or hurting each other."

My sister sobs and Mom joins her on the floor. "You took him from me. And now, you're trying to take my sister. I won't let you do it again." The needle slips from her hand onto the floor.as the needle slips from her hand onto the floor.

"We got a call for security. A uniformed man enters, and I tilt my head toward them huddled beside me. Plastic skates under my bed and I hear the syringe hit the wall behind me.

"Simmeon," Mom says, pushing up from the floor. "I... think we're okay now. Thank you for coming."

"Are you sure, Kris? Is this—"

"Lennon, yes. My oldest." She extends her toward my sister and this time she accepts. She raises herself to stand beside Mom and puts her jean jacket on over her bloody T-shirt.

"My goodness, I haven't seen you in years, darlin.'"

My sister's face cringes.

"So, you're sure everything is okay?" he asks.

"It is. Emotions are high. You see my other daughter," Mom says, pointing to me, "is admitted here. Lennon drove all the way from Boston to see her." She smooths the flyways around her face, and pulls her hair over her shoulders. "My friend is bringing doughnuts to the unit. Why don't you grab a cup of coffee and stay a minute?"

The security guard looks at both Lennon and me, then back to Mom. "I can do that, you sure you're all good in here?"

"Yes, we'll be fine." Mom wraps her arm around the security guard's back to escort him from the room. "How're Page and the kids doing?"

"Oh, you know teenagers."

CHAPTER SIXTEEN

Olivia

Mom returns from the storage closet with a long-handled duster. I cower with her approach as she extends the tool over the head of my bed. The badges on her lanyard jangle in front of my scrunched face until a thud, signals the okay to untwist it. Mom's expression is one I recognize from building Legos and doing puzzles together. Her eyes point toward the tiled ceiling. The tip of her tongue rests between her teeth. With a firm whack, an object skates under my bed again.

She leans down and rears up, cupping something in her palm. A few steps to the counter and Mom plunks it into the sharps container, giving the lip a firm tap. The door pivots closed, and she inspects it as it revolves open on return.

Taylor bounces into the room. My friend's eyes widen with their grin as they nudge Aunt Tish. "I told you she felt better today."

Tish's grin stretches into her round cheeks. Taylor releases her grip on a paper bag, bulging with breakfast pastries , and it falls on my bedside table. The wheels squeak with their push. "Look here, gurl. We ain't got no quitters on this team." Flyaway strands bounce around the wire-rimmed sunglasses tucked in a mound of coils on their head. They steer the table within my reach. "You got this."

Taylor pans the room. Lennon stands against the wall still holding her stomach with her two fingers. Mom twists her tousled hair into a low ponytail. "What'd I miss?"

Flipping her palms to the ceiling, my sister asks, "Where were you?"

"I—Oh sh—. Did it go down?"

"Did *what* go down?" Aunt Tish asks.

"N—nothing," Taylor stammers. My sister cuts her eyes at them before crossing her arms over her chest.

"It was me," I say, rattling the rocks in my throat. A sludgy cough follows.

Tish flashes her eyes in Mom's direction. "What was you baby?"

"I told Mom we wanted to come home." I glare at the top of my sister's a head. "You think *everything* is about you. *Your* happiness. *Your* misery. *Your* safety. *Your* sanity."

Mom is at my bedside in two steps. She holds a straw to my lips and the cold quenches. "You don't owe anyone an explanation," she says. "That's my job. In my attempt to protect you both, but I only caused more heartache. Let me explain—"

Sucking on the straw, I shake my head no. "Lennon, I knew what was going on at Dad's. You pretend I was some baby, but I knew things were messy." I huff. "Hell, I'm the one who almost died at his house." My mother's lip tightens as she straightens her back, holding the cup with both hands. "I wanted to move in with him as much as you did. I thought it was the right thing to do and I looked forward to spending more time together. But it didn't take long for us to realize Dad wouldn't deliver on all his promises."

Standing with her back on the wall, Lennon uncrosses her arms to fiddle with the cut on her stomach again.

"We were just part of Peyton's Insta story. She got a ton of clout for taking in two girls who needed a 'stable' mother. She painted Mom as an unfit parent, to boost her own ratings." Mom tightens her grip on the cup, giving the ice a swirl. I take the sip on cue. "We struggled to find security there. We were surrounded by material riches, but we were completely alone. Our relationship strengthened during that time; it was a good move for us in that aspect. When we went home for Christmas, I told Mom how you saved my life, but I was afraid the next time it happened you wouldn't be able to." My fingers go limp to the coarse sheet again. "Of course, Mom was already sus."

"In English, please," Tish says, sitting on the corner sofa with her elbows resting on her thighs.

"Suspicious."

"How'd you know, Aunt Kris?" Taylor asks, placing their chin in their palms and shifting the rolling table from side to side.

"Even after Olivia moved to Hutch's house, I monitored her blood sugars from my phone. It was the only way I still felt connected to her. Watching her lifeline, brought me some comfort. The night she fell down the stairs, I could tell from the waveform she'd reached a critical low at a very odd hour. The readout showed a lot of turbulence followed by a sudden spike. It was clear she'd received a large dose of sugar."

Mom's best friend greets her at the bedside and wraps her arm around her shoulder. "How horrifying. Watching your child in a life-threatening situation from hundreds of miles away. And then you didn't even get a courtesy call from the other parent to explain."

Tears form in Mom's eyes, and she draws her bottom lip in with her teeth.

"After that happened, he told me he understood if I wanted to go back to live with Mom. I think he felt guilty for not being there."

"So, why didn't you go home?" Lennon asks, raising her eyes to meet mine.

"I didn't want us to be separated again." My throat burns as I take two ice chips from a spoon Aunt Tish offers.

"Mom knew Dad was mentally warping you. His rhetoric was designed to turn you against her." My voice thickens. "I—I don't think he meant to, but he was consumed with revenge after their divorce and Peyton fueled his rage. For her, it was about the attention. It made a great storyline for her fans while Dad fell into a hole he couldn't crawl out of." My sister spins her rings on her finger. Taylor continues to sway on the bedside table. "Because of Peyton's insecurities, Dad moved away from us. Then, she convinced him to make us leave Mom. All so she didn't have to be bothered with another woman in the picture." I force a swallow. "They alienated us from Mom. We felt it, but we were too young to put it into words."

"Sometimes our bodies speak for us. Illness, aches, pains, all of it can be a sign we're not managing emotions," Mom says.

"I knew you'd find a way to get us out together."

"And she jumped right into action to save you, didn't she?" Lennon asks, pushing off from the wall and taking a step toward the bed.

Mom steps toward her. "I was trying to save two sisters. Allowing only one of you to live with him, as the court ordered, was a disastrous scenario. Together, I had confidence you'd look out for each other. When things started to spiral for both of you, I had to change plans."

"It didn't give you the right to kill our only father!"

Scratching echoes from the bedside speaker and Tish's eyes dart toward the glass doors. "Vy! If you don't turn that squawk box off right now, I'll..."

Beep boop.

My tongue moves the ice around in my mouth, and I suck the water from every groove. "You're right. It didn't, but the person who committed that act wasn't the mother we knew and loved. She had a psychotic breakdown."

"You don't have to defend me, Liv. Lennon knows I had severe depression and anxiety after our custody hearing." Mom faces my sister. "She's heard me talk about this several times in my therapy sessions."

"The ones she never participated in," I say.

"Well, you talked so much, it was hard to tell if it was Mom's session or your own!"

Tears stream across Mom's flared nostrils. "Then you know how hard I'd fought trying to keep you from moving. I knew it wasn't going to be the scenario he'd painted. By the time the judge ruled, I was exhausted. From attorneys to nosey neighbors...everyone had an opinion about how I was handling our separation, but nobody really cared. It was a revenue stream of drama for them." Mom's arms fall to her side. "I couldn't function at work. My marriage was stressed. I wasn't sleeping...my mental state impacted everything in my life. And I couldn't break free of the negative thoughts."

Lennon returns to tracing the tiles with her toes.

Aunt Tish steps toward Lennon. "Your mother was in a treatment center for weeks after your father's death."

"I remember when Aunt Kris was away. Len was at my house every day," Taylor says.

"Yes, we all pitched in to help Grey while Kris was admitted to the facility. It was essential to get her healthy again. She needed to return to being the mother she once was, but her mental state wouldn't allow it," Tish says.

"It took a lot of work for me to forgive myself for what I'd done. It still does," Mom says. "I never knew I was capable of such evil." I touch Mom's elbow as she sobs into her hands.

"And then you just let your mother rot in prison for your sins." Lennon growls.

"That was all Roz's plan," Aunt Tish puts her hands on her hips and stands behind Mom. "Your grandmother wanted to be absolved of her guilt for choices she made as a parent. Your mama didn't have anything to do with that. And once Roz put it into action, there was no stopping that woman."

"I should have told you the truth about why RaRa was arrested," Mom says. "I just didn't know how to explain it. I underestimated your maturity." Mom takes a deep breath. "At the time you moved to college, you and I were in a pretty tense place. Anything I said pushed you in a different direction. I should have done more to stay in touch with you, but I respected your need for space. I see, now, avoiding these discussions has led you to prepare answers on your own. That's no way to live. I'm sorry, I haven't been there for you."

Lennon juts her chin forward. "I thought I was doing the right thing by pushing my grief away," she says. "I didn't want to keep hurting. Dad's been gone for five years now, why can't I get over it?"

"A parent's death is traumatic enough, but then we can reexperience that grief with other life events we wanted them to share with us," Tish says. "Your sadness has been masked by anger. It's not surprising it worsened after graduation and moving to college."

"I still miss him too," I say.

"What about you, then?" Lennon asks. "Why are you so sick? This is more than diabetes?"

"It's like Mom said, sometimes our bodies express our grief for us," I say, cupping my bony writs with my hand.

"I really thought Mom was hurting you. I came here to save you."

Mom looks at my sister. "Under the circumstances, I can understand why you'd say that, but I've never been a threat to my children."

"I know, it's just—"

"Is that what was about to 'go down'?" Tish asks.

Taylor's eyes widen looking at Len and then back to Tish. They shake their head. "Big heart, bad plans."

CHAPTER SEVENTEEN

Lennon

The bed reclines, and Olivia drifts back to sleep.

Mom tucks the top cover around my sister's chest and dabs ointment around the scabbed edges of her mouth. She smacks them together slowly. I'm relieved the tube is out of my sister's mouth, even if it means having to hear her version of reality. Mom motions for Aunt Tish and Taylor to monitor Liv. Tilting her head toward the unit, she says to me, "Will you walk with me?"

I glance at Olivia.

"We used to be close Len. I want that again."

A deep inhale fills my lungs. "Sure, let me put some shoes on."

Mom walks into the unit, and I lace my boots sitting on the sofa. She's right; we used to be best friends. Maybe I have let my thoughts twist the truth.

The smell of the freshly bleached countertops takes over my senses again. Mom taps the desk. "Vy, we're walking. Tish and Taylor are in the room."

My aunt catches me staring at her and adjusts her blunt-cut bangs along her forehead. I stutter. "Vy, I—"

"It's okay," she says, resting her hand on mine. "Let's catch up soon, okay? I want to tell you all about Uncle Weyman's last TDY in Barcelona."

"I'm sure it was incredible."

"Too spicy for my taste. And you can only eat so much paella—"

Mom leans over the counter and says, "Let me know when Dr. Katz comes to the unit. I want to talk to him about placement options before he writes discharge orders."

"You got it, Kris."

"And call the charge nurse phone if my student needs me to sign off on anything."

Vy's head bobs as she raises her hand in the air without looking.

Mom has a way of taking control of any situation, and people fall in line. They trust her to make the best decisions possible for the patients, the nurses, and...at home. But like all of us, I guess, she has a breaking point.

The double doors separate with our approach, and we enter a dark hall. Neither of us speak. Standing next to Mom in the elevator, my stomach plummets with each passing floor. I can't believe I just tried to jab her with a narcotic-filled needle. I'm officially a lunatic. I know she wouldn't harm Liv, but why is her body deteriorating?

The chime signals our arrival in the lobby, and the doors push open. I step right but feel Mom tug my elbow. "There's a courtyard this way," she says.

I follow her through the bland halls with teal green directions at every intersection. Each pointing visitors to the area that best meets their needs. Some are looking for their loved ones so they can take them home. Others are searching for the chapel. Mom swipes her badge through a scanner and her hip pushes against the metal bar.

"My little oasis," she says.

Only she would find beauty in such a depressing place. "I don't remember this hideout," I say, scanning the pebbled garden. "Olivia and I definitely would have snuck our midnight snacks out here."

"Yes, you would have," Mom says, giving a half-laugh. "The Serenity Garden is one of my favorite spots to take my breaks. Especially on these cool fall mornings." Mom positions herself at one of the metal tables and gazes at a flowing birdbath. "Well, this has been an interesting shift already."

"Mom, I—I thought Olivia was in danger. I didn't really think you would do anything to hurt her, but...I'm an idiot."

"You're passionate. I love that about you." Her hand rests on my knee. "Your father was too. I loved that about him, also." She squeezes my leg. "Both of you charge into any situation determined and wholehearted. For him, it was work and his children. For you, it's your music and your family. The world needs more enthusiastic leaders like you and your dad."

My heart sinks into my chest as my eyes trace tiny sand-colored rocks beneath me.

"The truth is: Olivia *is* in danger. But it's not from you or me," Mom says.

"What? Who's hurting her?" I ask, wiping the corner of my mouth with my finger.

"She has an eating disorder." Mom's voice trails off at the end as she tucks the inside of her cheek between her teeth.

"That's why she's here? I thought it was her blood sugars. Tish said she had a seizure and was choking when the ambulance arrived," I say.

"Yes, that's true, but it's because she's regulating her weight by manipulating her blood glucose. It's called diabulimia. It's a condition where diabetics, usually young women, let their blood sugar run high on purpose. This puts them into ketosis," Mom says.

I raise my head. "Keto. Like the diets we used to do in high school?"

Mom closes her eyes and nods. "Right, the ones that deplete nutrients from muscles in your body."

"But you said her blood sugar was low when she got to the hospital. This disorder sounds like it should have been too high."

"Diabulemics don't eat regularly because they have body dysmorphia," she says, looking at my scrunched forehead. "They think they're fat when they're actually underweight." I nod. "They skip their basal dose, the one that gives them a base layer of insulin throughout the day, and if they eat, they usually don't dose for it either. Their blood sugar stays high as a result. Do you remember the signs of high blood sugar?"

The young student in the unit flashes into my mind, and I feel like I misrepresented myself earlier. Mom has treated us like her nursing students for as long as I can remember, even though I never officially enrolled in her class. "Tired, thirsty, tingling fingers. Liv used to get really bad leg pains."

"Exactly, it's usually when they start to feel bad physically and sometimes emotionally, they decide to take insulin. Sometimes they get the dose right, sometimes they don't. They want their metabolism to stay high, so it usually just wants enough medicine to end the painful side effects."

My eyes roll upward. "So, she wasn't eating, but she was probably having pain, so she dosed insulin, which bottomed her out. She overcorrected, basically." Mom confirms my statement with a nod. "It sounds awful. She's an athlete, she's funny, popular...why would she do that to herself?"

"Eating disorders can be a trauma response. Losing her father was an earthshattering tragedy. It's hard to say if she fully processed it when she was younger." She pulls her lip in. "Also, these things are usually about regaining control of something in the person's life."

"How so?"

"Diabetics are thrown into a world of carbohydrate counting, macro measuring, and constantly thinking about food. They often feel the pressure of making life sustaining decisions every minute of the day. While their friends are shoving Skittles and soda down their throats, insulin-dependent kids are forced to think like a human organ. Then, they have to live with the consequence of their action: if there's too little insulin, their bodies cripple. With too much insulin, they can starve their brains into a life-threatening coma. And even when they take their insulin on time, eating the right foods, exercising regularly...it doesn't always work. Their bodies are not their own."

"So, the dia-bul-i-mia." Mom's reassuring smile encourages me to continue. "It's a matter of Liv saying she eats what she wants, when she wants, and she controls the amount of medication she gives herself." Mom nods again. "How long has she done this?" I ask.

"A year, maybe two. It was easy to hide since she's so active. Any weight loss we noticed, we attributed to her intense schedule."

"How'd you find out?"

Mom straightens her back, pulling her shoulders back, then readjusts her ponytail she threw up when we got here. "Liv knew I struggled with eating disorders when I was younger." The pictures from the scrapbook flash through my mind. There were several where Mom's cheeks were round, and her tennis arms were sculpted. In others, she was flat, empty like my sister upstairs. "I'd picked up on a few signs. When I confronted her, it didn't take much for her to confess."

"Why didn't she tell me?"

"Only she can answer that. I'm sure it's not something she's proud of."

"Is she getting help?"

"She's had success with counseling, but it's not easy to break the cycle. It's been much worse over the past year."

"After I went to college."

"Nobody faults you for living your life." Mom leans toward me. "She, too, harbored a lot of unresolved guilt about your dad's death. I learned my mistake with not telling you the truth and made sure not to do the same for Olivia. Can we chalk it up to you being the first child?"

I shrug my shoulders.

"Once you heard the truth from RaRa, you pulled away from me. I knew I'd missed my opportunity to ask for forgiveness." She stares at the cream-colored pebbles beneath her feet. "When Liv started to ask questions, I shared the truth with her about my involvement. It helped her grieve. She's gone through a lot of therapy to help her process it. I should have told you the details before your visit to see RaRa, but I couldn't find the words. I'm sorry."

I force a swallow.

"As Liv grew older, she understood RaRa's willingness to own the guilty verdict. She knows my difficulties with accepting my mother's fate. Your sister's been completely open with me, and she's never mentioned you were a stress to her. If anything, you're the reason she wants to get stronger."

Mom stretches her hand across the wrought iron table to meet mine. I stare at the creases of her open palm but I can't muster the forgiveness to hold it. A cough forces my tightening throat open. "I told Liv we have a lot of crazy things to make up for. I've been absent for the past year, dealing with my own sh—issues." Mom folds her hand and rests it on her lap. "Upstairs, you told Vy you wanted to talk to the doc about placement options. What's that?"

"Your sister needs intense therapy. As much as I want to help her, this is more than I can guide her through. And her needs are more than the outpatient clinic can manage." Mom stands up, wiping the dust from her pants legs with both hands. "There's a specialty center for teens with medical disorders in Birmingham. They will help her with the underlying behavioral issues she's having and manage her diabetes."

"How long will she have to stay there?" Taylor asks.

"A couple of months. More or less," Mom says, looking at the cell phone buzzing from her hip. "Let me grab this, it might be about Liv."

Her voice stays low, and I hold my head in my hands. How could I—we have missed the signs? I assumed because she was so young when our lives crumbled, she'd forget the trauma somehow, but she's hurting. Just like me.

Mom returns to the table, "It's Dr. Katz. I'm going to run upstairs and meet him. He agrees with my request. Take your time coming back to the room. When you get there, we'll all need to tell Liv the plan and show our support."

"How do you think she'll take it?" I ask.

"She won't love the idea because it forces her to lose control again. But she'll accept it and, ultimately, kick ass." Mom winks. "You're a lot alike."

EPILOGUE

Lennon

Sweet smells of our holiday feast waft through Aunt Vy's house.

Olivia and I sit on the couch while an overweight Dachshund tugs at my shoelace. I swat the strings from his mouth. He nudges my leg until he loses interest and wobbles back to his owners in the kitchen. I scan the haul underneath the tree for boxes with mine and Liv's names, comparing the size of our gifts as I notice them. Multi-colored lights flicker around glass mementos from our aunt and uncle's travels, filling every perceivable spruce limb. The Eiffel tower, Tuscan cathedrals, and some from state-side attractions as well. A medallion-shaped ornament dangles from the branch close to me. Boston's cityscape is etched in the center, the date *2020* at the bottom. It's the year my father died. My muscles tense, but I sense the whisper for revenge and release it.

In the kitchen, Mom and Aunt Audrie critique their sister-in-law's cooking while sampling morsels from each dish. The Murphy brothers ease into the living room to size up their after-lunch spot for the football games later. Ches stands at the front window with his hands in his pockets. It's his typical holiday position. He's done it every year for as long as I can remember. A spectator in his child's life, he stood has and watched Taylor open everything from tricycles to her first car. I deepen my breathing to match his, knowing how it feels see everyone's lives move forward while yours stands still.

Removing his hands from his pockets, he pushes his chest out and steps to the door. "Hi, sweetheart," he says, opening it wide for Aunt Tish to walk through.

She's wearing a full-length red velvet jacket which is more than what's required for a walk across the street on a mild Christmas Day. The bell cut sleeves flare with her extended arms. His eyes move up and down her long frame, to the steamy casserole dish she holds in his direction. Taking the plate from her hands, he dangles a fresh sprig of mistletoe above her head. Tish leans in for a kiss.

"I'm sorry, we're late," she says, flipping her lush bangs across her forehead. "That child of yours tests my spirit even on the Lord's birthday."

Ches grins. "It's fine. Vy's still putting the finishing touches on the ham." He steals another kiss, and my body warms. "Where's our troublemaker?" he asks, walking over to add the dish with the others.

Tish glances over her shoulder, and I hear my friend's Docs scrubbing across the driveway. "Oh, hi, girls. I didn't see you there," Tish says, stepping inside. "Where's your mama?"

"In there," I say, nodding my head toward the kitchen. "What'd you bring?"

"Only your favorite." Tish shoots me and Olivia a wink, removing her long arms from each opening of her cape and draping it over a nearby chair. "Mama Rose's sweet potato shuffle."

My mouth waters thinking about the caramelized crunch of the first bite. Shuffle was Dad's favorite too. At night, he and I'd sneak into the refrigerator while the house was sleeping and finish off the leftovers. I hope he and Papa Kirby are sharing leftovers today. His best friend and role model, stripped too soon from his life as mine was. Hopefully, Dad's somewhere he can be himself: a place where he can eat sugar-coated potatoes in his concert t-shirt, talking about the biggest fish he caught with PaPa Kirby's fishing pole. A place so removed from life's pressures, bitter exes, and constantly falling short of his wife's desired social status. In some ways, I feel like he's a better father to me now. Loving me without the confines of Peyton's public measuring stick. A shiver runs down my spine and I know he's wrapping his arms around me right now. It's a feeling that comes over me when I'm showcasing a new musical piece I wrote or watching the Three Stooges on my phone at night before going to bed. It's a tingle I recognize and immediately know he's hugging me anytime he wants, not just when someone is taking a photo of us.

"Moms, what is in this box?" Taylor grunts.

"It's a gift for our hosts."

"Did you get the travel grill I told you to get?" Ches asks, returning to help Taylor position the box safely under the tree. "I know Weyman's been eyeing them at the store."

Tish's lip gloss shimmers in the reflection as she smiles watching him take the heavy load from their exhausted messenger. "I did, it's a good idea, baby." They gush at each other, and Taylor pushes through the space between them to join us on the couch.

Before the two can kiss again, a shout comes from the kitchen. "Tish, get in here and stop your husband from 'taste testing' the whole meal before we even sit at the table," Mom says, her head peers around the kitchen door and she blows me a kiss.

"Cheshire," Tish says, squeezing his cheeks gently with her hand. "You haven't taken your Pepcid yet."

Next to me, my sister flips through the scrapbook in her lap, pointing out my acne at every opportunity. Her hearty laugh warms me. A hint of pink flashes across her round cheeks as she tosses her golden ponytail over her shoulder, leaving it to dangle down her back. Her shoulders are rounded, not bony. Her rose-gold sweater folds along her back and the ridges of her spine are barely visible.

Mom told me she's graduated into an outpatient program and is living back at home. Although she's not medically cleared to start practicing again, she dresses out with her team and is their biggest cheerleader. Mom thinks she'll be able to make tennis season in the spring, and she's a likely candidate for the senior homecoming court. "Liv," Grey says. "I'm gonna need you to run that ten-and-out screen we used on them last year. Higgs can't keep up and Lennon, well..."

"I'm literally right here."

"I got you, G," Olivia says, raising her fingers in front of her face. "These hands are like mitts."

"I might surprise you," I say. "Taylor and I went to two football games this season." I hold two fingers up for the room to see.

"Olivia and I have a better passing game than any Ivy League team." The duo high-five each other. And I throw my Doc Marten over my knee, noticing my friend's are a perfect match. We give each other a nudge.

Uncle Higgs passes by the couch where we're sitting. "Don't let them bully us, Leonard. We've got some surprise routes up our sleeves too." I nod, feeling winded just thinking about running after lunch. "We may need to have you change your shoes, though."

I huff.

Our family gathers in the kitchen, forming a circle. Hand in hand, we huddle together like we have nearly every year for almost two decades. Tish's head bows deep, and she rests her hand on her husband's shoulder. She shares gratitude for our triumphs throughout the year while, per my usual, I look around the room at our group.

With their eyes closed and arms outstretched, I can their faces seemingly feeling whole. Accepting my own faults means accepting theirs. We aren't perfect, but there is peace in forgiving ourselves for falling short of an unachievable standard. It's a measuring tape held by the elite rich or anonymous social media mogul that makes us stumble. When we know any image portraying life as anything but messy is simply a filter.

Mom was right. Solace comes with death's end. It may of the end of a bad habit, the final word of a prayer, or the release of a grudge. Intertwined with other imperfect people, the wrath that left me battered, but not broken, washes through me. In the darkest hour, peace takes over turmoil and the sweet grace of its death allows my lungs to expand.

***

Acknowledgments

I must first thank the readers of my debut novel, *They Can't Eat You for Supper*. Without your interest, there'd be no need for additional books. I'm eternally grateful for your feedback and encouragement to keep writing.

Thank you to my husband who has offered his ongoing support during late nights and early mornings as I poured my heart into another novel.

To my high school best friend, Page, thank you for never forgetting I promised to write a spin off and holding me to that commitment.

To the creative talent whose helped me develop, edit, and format my books: without you, this hobby wouldn't be nearly as enjoyable. I send sincere appreciation to the beta readers who offered their honest critiques. To my editors, Edit My Novel and Let's Get Proofed, I'm humbled by your feedback and grateful for your exquisitely keen eye. To all contributors, thank you for sharing your time and talents.

And to my daughters who understand creative expression is the highest form of vulnerability, thank you for living in your truth and inspiring others to do the same.

About the Author

Roxanne's passion for writing started early in life thanks to her mother's encouragement. Today, she lives in the Southeastern US with her husband. They enjoy spending time with their three daughters and three dogs.

Thanks for reading! Please add a short review at your retailer's site and let me know what you thought!

Also by Roxanne Remy

They Can't Eat You for Supper
They Didn't Eat Me for Supper

Watch for more at https://www.roxanneremy.com.

Lightning Source UK Ltd.
Milton Keynes UK
UKHW040739160223
417122UK00003B/474